PRAISE FOR MIA HEINTZELMAN

PRAISE FOR MIXED SIGNALS

I0596196

Mixed Signals is funny, snarky, and heart warming romance that I couldn't put down. I can't wait for the next book in the series.

— AUTHOR D.W. MARSHALL

I also liked the humor in the book, and the author's writing style was enjoyable.

— AMAZON

There's no mixed feelings on this one, I'm glad I read it.

— AMAZON

Cute. Cute. Cute. This sent me into a tailspin. Think zombie but instead of brains, I wanted more books like this one. Cute with a bit of spice, and all things naughty and nice.

— GOODREADS

Mixed Signals was an unexpected surprise for me.

— GOODREADS

Enemies to lovers is my favorite troupe and this one just rocks it! If you like hate at first site books with convincing plot, great characters, hilarious banter, an uptight heroine, a swoon worthy hero, then please go for it. It was an enjoyable read and I like it a lot!

— GOODREADS

PRAISE FOR MIXED MATCH

This story had humor, heart, and heat and also made me hungry =).

— AMAZON

This is classic chick-lit with beautiful poetic passages and a hero and heroine you can root for. I highly recommend it.

— AMAZON

You know from the very beginning; this is a recipe for disaster without recovery and wonder these two can come out of this unscathed. I enjoyed the premise of this story and the journey to forgiveness and healing.

— MIDNIGHTACE BOOK BAR

I couldn't wait for this book to go live! I had the opportunity to read an ARC of Mixed Match and I loved it. There is a perfect balance of romantic tension, well meaning friends, love on the rise. Add to that a sexy hot guy and a leading lady with important decisions to make about her career and her heart and I couldn't stop reading. I can't wait for the next book in this series.

— AUTHOR, D.W. MARSHALL

PRAISE FOR MIXED EMOTIONS

I thought this book was a page turner as soon as I started reading it. If you are looking for a great romance novel, I'd definitely recommend this one!

— AMAZON

Tastefully done love scenes, just enough tension between "friends", humor, drama and all the things that we love when reading romance.

— AMAZON

I just wrapped up Mixed Emotions and Heintzelman officially has a new fan! This was the perfect mix of spicy, sweet, and a little bit of heat! Zora and Mike both are such likable characters and I love the friendship embedded deep into their relationship. I was drawn in from the beginning, with this being the easy-going, jovial read I needed this week. I'm a sucker for a friends-to-lovers romance and this hit the spot!

— AMAZON

PRAISE FOR WRAPPED UP IN BEAU

Perfect for the holiday season.

Perfect if you need a quick respite from holiday stress.

ALSO FROM MIA HEINTZELMAN

THE ALL MIXED UP SERIES

(Each book can be read as a standalone)

Mixed Signals

Mixed Match

Mixed Emotions

All mixed up - the series

STANDALONES

It's Got A Ring To It - Releasing 2021

HOLIDAY ROMANCE

Wrapped up in beau - Now in Paperback!

Married & Bright

Mingle All The Way

DARK ROMANCE

Devastated: Wastelands Academy Book 1

The Stacks w/a Emmaline Zanthi

Ruined: wastelands academy book 2 - releasing 2021

MINGLE ALL THE WAY

MIA HEINTZELMAN

LeviLynn

MINGLE ALL

THE

A NOVELLA

WAY

MIA HEINTZELMAN

Levi Lynn Books can bring authors to your live event. For more information or to book an event, visit our website at www.miaheintzelman.com.

Editing by Danielle Acee and Danylle Salinas

Cover design and Formatting by Tangled Covers

Manufactured in the United States of America

Cataloguing-in-Publication Data

ISBN 978-1-7359788-2-6 (trade pbk.) | ISBN 978-1-7359788-1-9 (ebook)

Name: Heintzelman, Mia, author.

Title: Mingle All the Way / Mia Heintzelman

Description: Mia Heintzelman | Las Vegas: Mia Heintzelman, 2020.

Subjects: Romance | Humorous fiction| Holiday romance.

To Daniel Heintzelman
Get the peanut butter whiskey shots ready.

CHAPTER ONE

"**H**ave ye no fear. She has arrived!" I sing, twirling over to my best friend, co-worker, and general event planning badass who's standing at a table at the back of the room. Nina is petite—barely up to my shoulder—and her thick, dark brown hair is in a perky ponytail. She's completely adorable. Also, I would do anything for her.

"Where do you need me? I brought a stopwatch—" I give the top button a click. It's responding ping is about as chipper as I am. "Just in case, I also brought my game face. This is Vegas. We can't be too careful."

Her perfectly micro-bladed brows dance as she gives me a quick once-over from my fabulous black thigh-high boots to my fierce red shift dress.

"*Yesss.*" She draws the word out, matching my dramatics with a snap of her fingers.

Nina darts her sparkly brown eyes over my shoulder as she tucks a glossy chestnut strand behind her ear. She leans in for a cheek-to-boob hug. Her cheek, my boob. *She's fun-sized.* I'm somewhere in between leggy volleyball player and WNBA player, though I am horizontally challenged. But, I digress.

I'm not here for men.

Just because I sell happily-ever-afters for the Lovestruck dating app doesn't mean it's a guaranteed employee benefit.

"She *is* ready. Red lips will do it every time," Nina continues.

"Bliss & Makeup Co. This is Crimson Queen," I say, filling her in on the best makeup to hit melanated girls since…ever. "Do yourself a favor and get one." I pucker, give her a shoulder shimmy and toss her a sweet smile.

She knows I'm not here to play around with these fools. This lipstick is all the drama allowed tonight.

"Girl, I've got this. Eight minutes sharp…like clockwork." I click the stopwatch button again for effect then whip my faux locs over my shoulder to the long line of bistro tables with flickering candles. Giant red Mylar heart balloons are strung with mistletoe over each two-seater table. "I'll usher the singles in. You'll do your little spiel, then the timed dates start. After, they'll have thirty minutes to mingle and fill out their little 'Let's make sparks' cards before I shuffle them out into the hands of the press for interviews."

I have a megawatt smile and arch a brow at her like, *they aren't even ready for all this, here.*

Nina's face twists with concern.

"What? You think they need more than half an hour to mingle?" I ask, failing to see the error in my plan.

It's the weekend after Thanksgiving. Technically, it's Small Business Saturday. No one is going to do anything to mess up the fat bonus coming my way when Nina pulls this event off. My plan is foolproof. Everyone who's anyone in Vegas is talking about it, and the PR companies are set to dutifully rave about it. When they do, ad sales on Cyber Monday will shoot through the roof, and Spencer James will be so thrilled, he'll gift everyone at Lovestruck financial tokens of his appreciation.

It's a no-brainer.

So, tonight there will be speed dating at this Lovestruck signature Mix'n'Mingle, but I will also duck and dive in and out of shadows to ensure things go off without a hitch.

When Nina doesn't verbalize what's screwing her face into a panic-stricken mess, my Spidey senses go off.

"Seriously, what?" I ask again. "Are you nervous? Did some guy already corner you? Because—"

"No. Nothing like that..." Nina's voice dies off, and I'm slightly relieved. These dating events can be dangerous for women in the game.

I don't know where men drew this conclusion, but for some reason, they think we're like some hyper-sexualized beings who love it when sleazy people aggressively "flirt" or demand reasons why we *shockingly*, don't want a second date.

Yeah, we love it when you make us feel unsafe in the name of love.

I have nothing against policing a bunch of people scheming for Christmas party plus-ones this time of year, but some people need to learn how to keep it classy.

That's what I'm here for.

"Actually..." Nina continues.

I busy myself tugging at the hem of my dress. I'm only halfway listening now because I've spotted the festive-looking open bar— my other excuse for showing up at a work event on my off day.

"Riley," Nina says my name flatly, which gets my attention.

"Yeah?"

"Change of plans. I need you in a *slightly* different capacity..." Her tense smile looks like it might snap at any second.

"Okaaay..." I drag the word out as I cock my head and narrow my gaze.

"Uh..." She scrunches her freckled nose and peeks an eye open. She's literally shaking in her open-toe booties. "The host from the speed-dating company has got all this stuff covered, so I don't actually need you to help *with* the speed dates. I need you to *be* a speed date."

See? I should've known this was too good to be true. My shoulders sag, and my head falls back as I groan. "What the heck, Nina? You know how I feel about dating in general. What makes you think I want to go on a dozen eight-minute dates all in one night? That's

3

ninety-six excruciating minutes of hell for me. You do realize that, right?"

She sighs, and her big, pleading, puppy dog eyes land on me with full force. "It's the holidays," she whines. "You won't have to do the mingle part or the interviews. Two people canceled, and I don't have an even number for the rotations."

This time it's me who sighs—a massive, throaty, full chest heave. Then my thoughts snag on the first part of that sentence. *Two people.*

"Wait." My posture is ramrod straight now. I square my body to Nina and lean down to meet her eyes. "Who else did you get to fill in?"

No sooner is the question out of my mouth when I have my answer.

Chase Campbell from web development bounds through the double doors with a cocky half-grin and perfectly groomed beard. He looks like he ripped his fashion sense right out *GQ*'s Best-Dressed Men of the Week—the Irish edition. He's tall, muscly, and lean with carefree product-whipped red hair. He's also incredibly annoying because he knows he's gorgeous. *Ugh.* Of their own accord, my eyes take in his cuffed dark jeans and perfectly rumpled military-style green jacket, which I'm guessing is his version of no-fuss casual.

There's nothing subtle about the man wearing the prep-meets-free-spirit clothes, though.

Which is why I always ignore him.

Quickly, I avert my gaze and resort to fidgeting with my cuticles. I'm not part of the Chase Campbell fan club. I leave that to the girls in the marketing department.

Holidays or not, I'm not about to switch it up.

"ALL RIGHT. SO, WHERE DO YOU NEED ME? I ASK.

Nina York flashes me a nervous smile. "Thank you so much for coming on such short notice, Chase. I'm totally going to owe you one." She shifts her body away from Riley Mills, whose tight red smile is fraying around the edges.

"Really. It's no problem. I'm happy to help," I say. I swear I hear a snort come from Riley, so reluctantly I tilt my head to meet Riley's steely gaze, careful not to gawk. "Hey, Riley."

She's tall with sculpted curves, long, shiny locs, and rich, dark skin. She's stunning in a way that always leaves me feeling blind-sided, but she's also a serious suit in the most severe sense of the word—all day, every day. She doesn't even take off her jacket at the office despite the casual environment at the Lovestruck head-quarters. At first, I thought it was because the A/C is always on high, but someone told me she lives by the "dress for the position you want" motto. Tonight, she must be throwing all that to the wind. The bare skin of her thighs that shows under the hem of her dress to the top of her boots...

The sight makes my stomach clench and sends a jolt right down to my dick.

Down, Chase. Barking up the wrong tree, here.

I swallow and avert my gaze because the reality is, I'm prob-ably the last person Riley Mills expected to see tonight. I can tell the surprise isn't a welcome one.

The Lovestruck office is an open-air industrial building with strategically clumped cubicles meant to section off departments. She's in sales near event planning and marketing at the front of the building, and I'm in IT and web development way in the back by the emergency exit, which I've contemplated using on more than one occasion—anything to avoid passing her desk and the inevitable pursed-lip death stare she seems to reserve just for me.

Not that I have any clue why...

Even if it always looks like it kills her, we try to exchange minimal words—real gems like "hi," "hello," and "thanks for holding the door," which is usually growled. Other than those rare pleasantries, she seems to loathe me for reasons I'm still unaware. For her part, I suspect she interacts with me out of courtesy and professionalism, mostly. For me, it's a combination of fear and self-preservation, which is why I avoid her like the beautiful, bronze goddess plague that she is to my ego.

Nina clears her throat and flashes Riley a pointed stare. In an unexpected twist, Riley says, "Hi." It's like pulling teeth.

Now that wasn't so hard, was it?

Nina bounces up on her toes, breaking up the whole three-word conversation.

"So…" she rests her hands on my shoulders and lowers her chin before blurting out. "I need you to be one of the speed daters."

Oh, fuck. Why?

My gaze slides to Riley who crosses her arms over her chest and shakes her head. Right, she's been asked to be a date, too. So, somewhere in the rotation, Riley and I will be face to face for eight minutes.

In my book, that's plenty of time to get to the bottom of her apparent hatred for me.

Thanks, Nina.

"Yeah, I'm good. Whatever you need," I say with a shrug, doing my best to sound breezy and unaffected. On the inside, however, I'm rubbing my hands together at this twisted conspiracy Nina cooked up for us.

Or did she? Why would she?

Precisely ten minutes later, Nina and some young kid she has doing her gopher work let the singles in, and she gives her perky introduction speech, which is a bubbly welcome and thank you. Then she gives the rules of the event along with a warning about what would constitute dismissal from this event and all future events put on by Lovestruck. *Whoa, I guess she's not messing around.*

Half an hour later, I'm three dates in, two away from Riley, and I catch her sneaking glances over at me. I shoot her a confused look in return. That earns me a smile, which only makes my anticipation of our eight minutes together that much stronger.

Then, we're one table apart. She's with a typical tall, dark, and tattooed guy who is talking about his fitness training business, and I am with a raven-haired CEO who keeps going on about washi tape. *Whatever that is.* Much to my relief, Riley looks bored out of her mind.

When the timer goes off, and I switch into the chair in front of Riley, I go for it. "Want to tell me why you've been giving me the evil eye since date two?" I ask. *Oh, yeah, I'm going for it.*

She shakes her head and smiles. Maybe it's the candlelight flickering off her rich brown skin, or the way it glints off her eyes and turns them a warm shade of amber, but I'm mesmerized. I'm charmed by the prospect of graduating to two-word exchanges.

"Why are you even here? Isn't one of the marketing girls free tonight?" she asks with an eye roll.

Okay, a whole string of words. We're getting somewhere.

"Is that why you hate me?"

She presses a finger to her temple and massages like talking to me is *so* stressful. "Oh, your ego isn't massive or anything. Relax. Not everything is about you, believe me. I was just commenting on our work prospects. That's all." She presses the air with her palms.

There's something telling about the way she keeps looking away.

"Maybe, you don't hate me...because you like me." I cock my head to read her reaction.

"I don't date. Period."

So, you agree. You do like me.

I nod, and the corners of my mouth tug downward as my lower lip protrudes. "Wow. So, what's this we're doing?" I lean in, forcing her gaze, and whisper, "It sort of feels like a date."

She parts her lips then closes them again.

"Just the facts." I shrug and lean back against my chair.

"I'm here as a favor to Nina just like you are, so save it. *And* there are free drinks. Don't go reading more into it." She runs a hand over the long black coiled strands of her hair. Then she surprises me. "I don't care how many minutes each date is, it's

7

just nice to see a familiar face and have an unscripted conversation."

"So, you agree. It's nice to see my face..." I'm bobbing my head, biting back a shit-eating grin as a warm, musical laugh pipes out of her. I love this new unexpected banter between us. It's like we've been in the middle of a conversation all this time, and we've just jumped back in where we left off.

Then, the host, a tall, boisterous woman in a black jumpsuit with short platinum-blonde hair eases up to our table and positions the mic inches from her neon pink lips. "I want to pause for a few seconds. Go ahead. Stop the clock!" She gestures to Nina, who is all too happy to hear what the woman has to say.

The host flips the mic between Riley and me. "What are your names?"

We both hesitate, but eventually cave and tell her.

"Now, I don't mean to put you on the spot..." *Oh, sure you do.* "But I want everyone to stop what they're doing and take a look at Chase and Riley. They just met, what, four minutes and twenty-three seconds ago? Just like you. But I'll tell you a little secret. These two...they have it."

The room erupts into applause. Every pair of eyes in the place is on us. Honestly, I'm right there with this woman's assessment. She's not lying. The hair on my arms and the nape of my neck is raised. My heart is fluttering in my chest. I'm aching to reach across and touch Riley...or for her to touch me.

A slow smile tugs at the corners of my mouth until I see Riley's expression. She's tense. Her eyes dart to the host before landing—hard as bricks—on me.

"When the clock is ticking," the host continues, putting us directly on the spot despite the murder in Riley's eyes, "you can't get to know a person by asking their favorite color and what they do for a living. Questionnaires do not a connection make. You have to jump all the way in. These two are in each other's face, asking questions, smiling—I'm talking fierce eye contact, hair-touching, lips parted, leaning in. Yes, to all of it! The heat between these two is combustible."

In exactly this moment, I realize three fundamental truths. One, by the intensity of Riley's reaction, whatever this loathe-hate thing is, the feelings between us aren't one-sided. Two, the ache to touch her has spread to the growing hard-on in my pants. And three, the pursed-lip death stare is going to be epic on Monday.

CHAPTER TWO

I'm supposed to be in my cubicle by eight, but I slip in the door past a dozen people and over to Nina's desk five minutes late...on purpose.

"What's going on?" I ask, ducking below her wall.

Every person from IT, HR, accounting, and marketing is walking toward the front of the building in droves, which is exactly what I don't want. I always avoid Chase Campbell, but after Saturday and the speed date event, the plan is not to take any chances. Show up late so there's no time for chitchat or for him to hold the main door, even when I slow down so he can go first. I even packed a soggy peanut butter and jelly sandwich to eat at my desk so I wouldn't have to see him in the lunchroom.

"Spencer James called an all-hands meeting," Nina says, locking her computer.

"Shit. Do you think he saw me come in late? Think it's about a holiday bonus?" I'm talking a mile a minute.

Nina shoots a confused glance at me. *Damn. Chase has me on edge.* I'm plastered against the gray fabric of her wall about to knock down the thumbtacks holding up her Men of New York calendar. "What are you doing?"

"Shh. Hiding."

"From?"

As more people pass the cubicle, I peek over the top of the wall only to catch Chase's baby blue eyes before I drop to the floor. "Dammit."

On cue, he appears at the entrance of Nina's cube wearing a pair of low hanging jeans and a black Henley pushed up at the sleeves. His outfit makes my pulse quicken. Almost instantly, I regret crawling around on my hands and knees pretending to be searching for Lord knows what on Nina's floor—even if it's the perfect position for what my lady flower needs to get out of a self-imposed drought.

Holy wet dream.

"Found it," I say, popping up and tucking my empty hand into my pants pocket. "Oh, hey."

His brows furrow, but then he shrugs it off. "I was hoping I could walk with you guys to the meeting. Any idea what this is all about?"

"A bonus, I hope," I say.

The three of us walk out into the aisle and I can feel Chase's arm hairs brush against mine like flint and steel, striking up sparks he has no business igniting. *Gah, he's such a fucking tease.*

Nina leans in squishing me further into him. "I heard Jessica Faulkner telling someone Eric Voorhees was leaving—"

"Shut *up*." I slap my hand over my mouth.

Chase sighs as if it's too much to have an actual shocked reaction. *Sorry, we aren't your regular group of swooning women from marketing.*

"If that's true, there's going to be movement," he says.

"And you know Jessica's going to be the first one all up in Spencer James' face with muffins or good coffee or something equally obnoxious. She's such a freaking suck-up." I roll my eyes. "I love the name Jessica, but she's totally ruined it for me."

Chase and Nina look at me like I've sprouted horns.

"Anyway, I was waiting for a little later in my five-year plan, but if it's true, I'm going to go for it. I have so many ideas to make us competitive in the dating industry—and safe for women."

Chase's vibrant eyes snap to mine like he's just put together a piece of the puzzle that is the mystery of Riley Mills.

I wave off his empathetic stare and hang a step back so I can see through the haze. "For everyone, really. I mean, like, more safety features. It would mean combining the best and safest features of online dating services, meet groups, spark networks, and match groups."

Surprisingly, he nods, and I'm inclined to continue.

"I'm just interested in giving people the best shot to find love."

Chase pulls his bottom lip between his teeth, and though I try not to stare, I am. It's embarrassing. Good God, he's so freaking hot. *But I will not be affected. I'm a professional.* Up close and in the warm indoor light, I can't *not* notice the constellation of freckles all over his face. Oh, and his piercing blue eyes are like supernovas exploding and shooting off flares that hit me straight in the vagina.

I press my hand to the nape of my neck and loosen the collar on my blouse. Then, he frees his lower lip.

Did it just get hotter in here?

"I'd love to hear about it. There are some features my team is working on for the app now we might be able to tweak. We could figure out how to implement your ideas."

My wretched heart gives a small lurch at his sweet smile.

This is all bad.

Then, everyone is assembled in a half-circle around Spencer James' front office. Quiet anticipation falls over the room, and the whispering stops.

Spencer's appearance is as exquisite as it is authoritative. Today, he's wearing a sharp navy blazer with pressed jeans and a white collared shirt that's unbuttoned at the top. A close-shaven black beard outlines his full lips. His skin looks as if it was molded from rich, dark earth and chiseled in the likeness of the gods. What I've always liked about him is that he isn't quick to wield his power. He's quiet and observant and takes the time to make eye contact with each and every waiting pair of eyes. He smiles warmly.

I've heard him speak at least quarterly, but I find I'm never prepared for his voice. He's got the trademark low baritone to fit his refined gentleman aesthetic. It's his easy croak between pauses —kind of like a pilot before takeoff—that makes me feel like he's about to guide us into unchartered territory.

So, I brace myself.

"Thank you all for stopping what you're doing to give me a few minutes of your time." He runs a hand over his bald head before standing taller and tugging the lapels of his blazer. "As many of you may have heard, our senior marketing manager, Eric Voorhees is no longer with the Lovestruck team."

A collection of gasps and sighs wash over the room.

"While one of our own leaving is a sad event, we wish him the best." He lifts his chin regally, and I'm holding my breath. "That leaves us with an opportunity, doesn't it?"

I can almost see the claws coming out and the blood in the water. A new position most likely means an internal promotion. I realize just at this moment I want it *badly*. While I've only been with this company three and half years, this could finally be my chance to put my sales and marketing degree to use.

My mind drifts to my sister Keira and so many young women like her, who should be able to date, find love, or have sex without the fear of being catfished *or nearly assaulted*.

I have to get this position.

"So, we're going to have our first annual holiday party December 18th. As we prepare our office for the holidays this week, it feels like the perfect time to show my appreciation. It'll give us a chance to say our goodbyes to Eric and give me a chance to mingle with all of you."

After the whispers and chatter die down and the crowds gradually disperse, I'm hoping to get Riley alone to talk about what happened Saturday and maybe explore what that look she gave me after we left Nina's cubicle was all about.

But Nina doesn't move.

And neither does Jessica Faulkner.

"Oh my gosh. Isn't this amazing?" she says turning to the three of us. "You know what this means…" When we all stare at her confused, Jessica relieves us of our suspense. "He's totally going to pick Eric's replacement at the holiday party. It's completely his MO."

Riley's top lip curls and I'm pretty certain she's on the verge of rolling her eyes at Jessica, so I interject and save her from herself.

"What makes you so sure?" I ask, genuinely interested in how she's unearthed some pattern between the open position and the holiday party.

Jessica, in her all-things-pink signature look, pushes her thick-rimmed pink glasses up the bridge of her perky nose like she's been waiting for someone to ask just this question. She straightens, catches a strand of her sandy blonde hair in her hand, and starts to twirl it around her finger. "Remember Lacey Anderson's birthday in the lunchroom when Spencer announced he was adding another event planner to the staff? Or the Fourth of July when he scooped up Darrell Jenkins from iMatch for the IT team?"

Both Nina and Riley nod.

"Spencer James is one hundred percent a big production guy. He likes fireworks and fanfare. When he makes an announcement, it's going to be huge."

Nina nips at the tip of her finger like she's weighing the conclusiveness of Jessica's supporting evidence.

"That *could* be the case," Riley says with slightly less disgust in her tone.

Then Jessica hits us with, "Plus, Eric totally said he'd put a good word in for me with Spence."

Now I'm at risk of rolling my eyes.

Because Jessica is so tight with Eric Voorhees and Spencer

James, they're on a first-name basis. *Give me a break.* Word about Jessica taking credit for Reyna's sales last year spread through the cubicles like wildfire. So, not only is she a brownnoser who's willing to sabotage, it looks like we can officially add office gossip to the growing list of reasons she is quite possibly the worst candidate for management.

As close as web development and marketing have to work together on this app, there's no way in hell I'm reporting to a woman who only wants the title and has no actual plans to make the company better. *Unlike, Riley...*

"That's awesome, Jess." *There's your first-name basis for you.* "I hear you might have some stiff competition, though."

Pure satisfaction oozes through my veins to see the panic flash across Jessica's face. "Why? What have you heard?" She swallows and leans in closer.

I toss Riley a glance before turning back to Jessica. "Just that Spence has pegged a diamond in the rough." I shrug.

Jessica folds her arms over her chest and narrows her big brown eyes at me. "Well, I hope whoever it is knows that Spence is notorious for picking sticky people. Everyone he's promoted over the *five* years I've been here has reasons to stick around—like a marriage and kids or a mortgage. Even a dog will do. He's not looking for someone who'll just up and decide to jump ship to a competitor."

Nina and Riley stand there tight-lipped, their eyes darting between Jessica and me like we're in a tennis match.

And the ball *is* in my court.

"That may be true." I tilt my head to the side, conceding the validity of her point. There isn't an employee at the Lovestruck headquarters who's been here under three years. "But he also wants people who are looking to make his company better. He likes taking chances, too...on people who are hardworking, and *ethical.*"

She gasps and holds her chest like I've struck her right in the heart. Her sweeping lashes flap like crazy. "Whatever, Chase," she says, open-mouthed. "I was just letting you guys in on what I know. Figured you'd be happy since we'll be working so closely when I get the position, but...no matter." She plasters on a smile and straightens her posture. "Hope you guys have a nice rest of the day."

The second she's out of earshot, Nina plants herself in front of me with the widest smile. Her dark ponytail is still swaying. "Well color me surprised. I didn't know you had it in you. *Damn.*"

Riley dips her chin and one shoulder to look at me from beneath her brow. She gives me a painstakingly slow stare down that leaves me throbbing in southernmost places that are not work appropriate. When her eyes reach mine, along with flecks of gold, there is light and amusement in her warm gaze.

"Where have you been hiding this hardcore badass all this time?"

I chuckle, and she matches me with an airy giggle.

"I mean, not that everyone didn't already know she was shady as heck, but dang. You put her business all out on front street." She laughs and latches onto my arm sending a ripple of heat racing through me. "And excuse me, who is this diamond in the rough who's going to save us from the suck-up?"

Without a hint of humor, I say, "You."

CHAPTER THREE

W e've barely inched into December and by Tuesday, the office is already in full holiday mode. Holly is draped over the tops of... Every. Single. Cubicle. Bright red poinsettias and fully dressed wreaths are strategically placed around the doors and edges of the open space. A cheery playlist of exactly one hundred of the most silver-jingle-bells-joy-to-the-Tannenbaum-chestnuts-roasting holiday songs is playing on a loop. And just off the entrance to Spencer James' glassed-in office is a gigantic ten-foot tree with a shiny star at the top.

It's pretty safe to say we're feeling the holiday spirit at Love-struck, but I can't exactly adopt the cheer just yet.

I slap my hand down on my knee to stop the bouncing and look up just as Jessica Faulkner leaves Spencer's office. My eyes dart from her pink newswoman dress to the large coffee and muffin on Spencer's desk then back to her easy stride as she flashes me a quick smile.

Bah humbug to you, Jessica.

"She's not going to get it even if she buys him a whole coffee shop and a bakery." Nina's head pops up over the top of my cubicle wall. "Go. Now."

I heave a heavy sigh and nod, wishing I'd stopped for good

coffee instead of the crappy lunchroom stuff. "You're right. I'm just going to go in there and tell him why I'm a good candidate for the position."

"Breathe. All this garland and merriment, he's probably in the best mood."

Dipping my hand in my locs, I scratch my scalp and blow out a breath.

"You got this. 'You are smart. You are kind. You are important,'" Nina says, mimicking *The Help* and making me laugh.

It's enough to get me on my feet. I grab my portfolio and march toward my goal. My future is just like the star on that tree—bright and at the top for a reason.

When I reach Spencer's office, I lightly tap on the glass, and he waves me in.

"Ah, Riley. This is a pleasure," he says, his voice cracking reassuringly.

This is the same guy who hired you. He knows what you're capable of and how hard you work. You're ready for this opportunity. And you're ethical, dammit.

"Thank you, Mr. James. I—"

"Spencer, please."

I swallow. "Oh. Okay. Thanks, Spencer. If you have a few minutes, I know you haven't stated when you plan to replace Eric Voorhees, or if you will at all, but I'd like to officially express my interest in the position when and if you decide to. I've only been here three and half years. I know that's not as long as—"

"Slow down. It's okay. I'm just another co-worker. No need to be nervous around me."

I breathe a sigh and give him a small smile.

He gestures to the two sleek metal armchairs facing his plexi-glass desk. "Please, join me."

Through the door, I hear Have Yourself a Merry Little Christmas playing over the loudspeaker—the Ella Fitzgerald version from all my favorite holiday movies. The light tinkling sound and the harmony of her silvery voice soothes my nerves just a little.

Spencer leans back against his chair and folds his arms. "So, tell me, have you made plans for the holiday? Started shopping for gifts yet?"

The questions catch me off guard. I sort of got the impression he was a straight-down-to-business guy.

"Yeah. My family's here in Vegas. They live over in Green Valley. We usually celebrate Christmas Eve. We open gifts right at midnight, then laze around on Christmas day. I'm pretty bad about shopping, though. I usually put it off until the very last minute," I say with a laugh.

"That sounds nice, actually."

For what feels like two full minutes, we say nothing. Just sit there in awkward silence. But then, he sits upright and clasps his large hands on the edge of the desk. His brow creases as he slowly blinks a dozen or so times.

"I hope you don't mind my asking, but…is there a reason you don't have pictures on your desk? Personal items? There's just a desk organizer and a calendar." His full lips purse as he lifts his chin to pin me with a stare. "Is it that you don't feel safe or comfortable displaying your private life, or is there something else?"

My mouth falls open, but nothing comes out.

Somehow, my actual explanation of being a neat freak and maintaining a professional space feels underwhelming and, pretty pathetic. I don't actually have anyone's picture to tack to the wall. I love my parents, but I don't need them watching me at work all day.

The memory of the day Spencer announced the party comes flooding back to me like a tsunami, pulling everything up by the roots.

All I can think about is Jessica's contention that he only promotes people in relationships, or with kids and mortgages. Maybe he changed the subject from the position to the holiday and family life because I'm not his ideal candidate. I'm single—no kids, no pet, no mortgage. I'm renting a super-cute chic little house in the northwest. I have the lowest tenure here. As far as he's seen, I'm basically the billboard for a flight risk.

"No, it's not that. I'm uh…"

I clear my throat and turn toward the glass at my right. There is Chase Campbell with a sweet smile, taking careful steps to avoid spilling the well-meaning crappy coffees he's carrying in each hand—one for him and likely one for a member of his all-female fan club in marketing.

And that's when the lightbulb goes off in my head.

"I'm in a serious relationship," I blurt out.

"Oh, well. Good for you." Spencer's face lights up and his chin lifts like the news of my fake relationship has infused him with a newfound interest in me. "I'm happy to hear it. Thank you for sharing."

A wave of adrenaline washes over me and I sit up, nodding. "It's just that he works here too—not in the same department though," I add, quickly. "So, I didn't think it was such a good idea to put his picture up on my desk."

Slow it down. Take a breath.

Under the clear desk, my knee starts bouncing again because I'm nervous, and also, I'm a *big fat liar*. But it's too late to take it back now.

I press my hand down hard on my knee to still it, and flash him a closed-mouth smile.

This is not one of those times when you can just say, *JK. I was just seeing how you'd react.* No take-backs. My heart pounds against my chest.

Boy, I have really done it this time.

MY PHONE PINGS BACK IMMEDIATELY.

Todd 9:43 am
So, what happened? Have you seen her since?

My brother, Todd, and I had been texting back and forth when I made the mistake of mentioning I'd been on a speed date. Now, despite having the perfect marriage, a kid on the way, and a dream job running a local all sci-fi bookstore, for some reason he feels the need to live vicariously through my love life.

I'm about to respond with some vague dismissal of the subject when I lift my chin and catch a sight of Nina's wide-eyed nervous expression. I follow her line of vision.

From back here in web development, I have the perfect view of Spencer James's office, so the glare off his swinging glass door as Riley Mills comes out speed-walking immediately snags my attention.

Shit.

I toss my phone aside and shoot Riley a thumbs up in question, thinking she's going to veer off to her cubicle, but she does not detour. Todd can wait. Her eyes are wide. Her neck is stretched tall. The further down the aisle she gets, the panic on her face comes in clear and in technicolor.

Then I realize she's on a straight path for me.

The fact she passes her own desk and beelines toward the back catches everyone's attention. Heads begin popping up over the walls. Apparently, they're all watching her too. Naturally, she gets the side-eye from Jessica who's put two and two together to figure out Riley is the "diamond in the rough."

When Riley reaches me, I flash her a hopeful smile. "How'd it go?"

She flits a glance at the coffee cup on my desk then at the one I left on Evelyn's from marketing—to return the favor—before grabbing my hand and dragging me to the exit where all the smokers take their breaks every fifteen minutes. As soon as we're outside, she gives the two people chilling along the wall her famous, and effective, death stare.

Warned, they quickly put out their cigarettes and duck back inside.

"What? It went that bad?" I ask once we're alone.

Riley starts fanning her hands and taking gulps of air. "Oh my god. Oh my god. Shit. I'm totally freaking out right now."

"Relax. You were in there for like twenty minutes. I'm sure it's going to be fine," I say, gently touching her arm.

Apparently, touching her is what it takes to calm her down because she stops with the flailing hands, and her whole body tenses.

"Sorry," I say instinctively.

"It's okay. I just...I told Spencer James we've been in a serious relationship for almost four years."

My mouth falls open. Then all the air in my chest vacuums out of me. "Why?" I scrub both hands over my face and drag them through my hair. "Why would you tell him that?"

I cannot close my mouth.

"It started off fine. I went in there and said I was interested in the position. But then he changed the subject to family and holiday shopping and why I didn't have pictures on my desk. I couldn't get Jessica's words out of my mind, so I figured, if he only promotes sticky people, I'd say I was in a serious relationship."

"Okay, I'm still not following where I come in."

"Not only do I want this in this worst way, but I also don't want Jessica to get the position. Can you imagine working for her?"

I pinch the bridge of my nose. "No, but when did you throw me into the mix?"

"Right. So, you walked by, and I got an idea. It seemed inno-cent enough to say I didn't have pictures because I was dating someone *at* Lovestruck in a different department. But then he asked who..."

"And you couldn't have said *anyone* else. What about Darrell or Caleb?"

I heave a sigh and start pacing the side of the building, but when I pivot to her again, it's back. The death stare.

"What?"

"Why Darrell or Caleb? Because they're black too?" She juts her chin out. Her tone is all vinegar, no honey. "I guess you and Renee or Charlotte are matches made in ginger heaven, then."

My stride is easy as I erase the distance between us. "It wasn't like that. I just meant, I know you're friends with those guys. I always see you talking and laughing with them. Let's be real here, the first time you've said more than two words to me was at the speed date event. Let's not act like we owe each other favors."

She takes a deep breath, which I'm guessing is her way of acknowledging my point. "Sorry. It wasn't fair to just lump you in with Renee and Charlotte. You're pretty cute for a gingy."

Every muscle in my body softens against her words—well, almost every muscle. "Cute, huh?"

"Anyway." She rolls her eyes playfully and her lashes sweep up in a flutter as she laughs. "You should've seen how Spencer lit up when I told him it was you."

"Really?" *Hmm.*

Riley arches a brow and the beginnings of a smile tug at the corners of her lips. "Yes. He said he wants me to bring you to the holiday party, and he'll keep me in mind for the position."

"Okay, so what's the plan then? How are we going to do this?"

She shoots me a megawatt smile. "So *we* are doing this?"

I nod even though I must be out of my mind. Everything can go wrong, but I'm helpless against those eyes...and those lips.

"For what it's worth, I didn't know if you'd agree, so I told Spencer we were keeping it low-key and professional for work purposes. All we have to do is shoot each other sweet smiles every once in a while, until the party when he announces his decision. I won't sneer at you. And you can bat your long lashes at me and make the marketing girls all jealous."

Riley peeks her tongue out to lick her lips and I'd pretty much say yes to anything she asks.

"Then," she starts, and I think it's going one way, but she says, "when the time is right, we'll stage a breakup."

It surprises me how my shoulders sag. What did I think she was going to say, we'll take things slowly? What things? We barely know each other. Still, she's got the ending figured out before we've even begun.

I'm going to need more time to downshift.

"You know, that's the second time you've brought up the marketing girls…" I say, buying myself some time.

Riley sinks her teeth into her full lower lip, a move that hasn't failed to make my dick twitch yet. She lifts her brows and smiles. "I dare you to tell me I'm wrong."

I dare you to tell me you haven't been watching me, too.

I take another step closer until there's only inches between us. In heels, Riley's top lip is aligned with my lower. If I wanted to, I could eliminate the whisper of a distance between us and taste her sweet heat. I could pull a deliciously sexy moan from her mouth and see what she'd think about playing with this fire between us then.

She's breathless. Her chest rises and falls to a quick staccato daring me to finish what she started.

Instead, I slide my hand to her waist and dip my hand in her jacket pocket where she stashes her phone. Then, as much as I hate being away from her heat, I step back. "Why don't we work on that picture for your desk?"

This is going to be fun.

CHAPTER FOUR

After that libido jumpstart he pulled by the side of the building with his face an inch from my mouth, we had an impromptu photoshoot, and the games began. I may have pressed my ass up against his completely impressive hard-on, but he started it when he banded his arms around me, wrapping me in his warm, spicy scent.

Where did this guy even come from? He always seemed sleazy and a little too…too something. Where's he been hiding his smooth, gentle, heat magnet side? And why am I just taking notice?

Why am I so caught up in this farce?

A week later, there are exactly two totally appropriate framed pictures of us on my desk. One is in a frame with the words "Joy to the World" at the top, with my back flush against his chest and his lips alarmingly close to my ear. It has definitely provided fodder for office gossip—joy for those with no business of their own to mind.

We're all anyone wants to talk about.

The second frame is more for my own amusement. As bad as I wanted Chase that day, I indeed felt like a Ho!Ho!Ho!

"Hey, babe, you ready to pack it in for the day?"

Chase glides his hand down my spine, and I may as well be naked by the way my skin blazes under his touch.

Focus, Riley. This is not real.

I jolt upright, correcting my posture and swivel to face him. "Logging off now, sweetums," I say, wishing I didn't feel as flustered as I'm sure I look.

A quick glance around the room reveals the office is almost cleared out for the day. Jessica and Charlotte are headed toward the exit, but the fact we're basically the last two people here doesn't exactly do the trick to ease my nerves.

In fact, as I slip on my pale blue peacoat, I feel the tension in my shoulders tighten. "Ready."

But then, just like every time Chase intertwines our fingers, I'm putty. My pulse picks up and a literal shiver runs over my body.

"Relax," he whispers then jerks his chin to Spencer's office. "He always stays late on Tuesdays."

I nod and do my best to even my breathing, but, dammit, Chase Campbell is beyond sexy in his black leather jacket. My mind keeps dragging me through images of him on a damn motorcycle telling me to climb on. I don't even like motorcycles. They're unsafe.

"Got it." I swallow and nod repeatedly, making the mistake of meeting his heated gaze.

Maybe I didn't think this fake relationship thing through.

And as far as hats go on guys, they're usually hit or miss. Especially this time of year when women can get duped by a guy who's seemingly hot until he removes his cap to reveal a misshapen head or a weirdly unbalanced forehead. But, my stars, Chase's strong bearded jaw with that little tweed ivy cap. *Phew.* It shades his steel blue eyes in a way that does wonders for my imagination—one more layer to remove with my teeth.

"Okay. He's watching so…I'm going to kiss you."

Alarms could be going off. Bombs could be dropping out of the sky. Hell, if I know. I can't hear a thing over the sound of my heartbeat pounding in my ears. *Kiss?*

His throat bobs.

"What, here? Now?"

"Preferably while he's got an uninterrupted view."

Chase scratches his beard. It's my mistake for looking because now I want to feel the roughness on my lips and run my fingers in it. *Between my thighs...* "Um..." My throat has closed up. I'm blinking like a wild banshee. *What the hell is a banshee, anyway? Do banshees even blink?* "Okay."

He leans in painstakingly slow, and I'm holding my breath because I'm not sure I won't faint. I close my eyes.

I hear a warm, throaty laugh from deep down.

When I flutter my eyes I open, the man is doubled over. "I got you so good," he says between chuckles.

My mouth falls open. *This fool...*

"But it's good to know you're game." He clears his throat. "The man said it was fine since we're in different departments, but I doubt he's good with us putting on a show right in front of him." *Obviously. Ugh.*

I shrug. "Not for nothing, but I was just seeing if *you'd* go along with it."

"Yeah, okay. Come on. Let's get out of here." Chase throws his arm over my shoulder and grabs my purse as we walk toward the exit. "You have an umbrella?"

"No. I'm good though. My car isn't far."

He's still biting back a laugh. "We can share. Mine's big enough..."

"Ha. Ha."

Chase tosses me a wink, and I want to be pissed. I *really* want to be, but it's kind of hard when he's so dang adorable. Plus, I'm the one who dragged him into this "relationship." He's just making the most of it—finding *all* the humor.

OUTSIDE THE COOL AIR LASSOES THE RAIN, WHIPPING IT AGAINST US AS I fumble to open up my umbrella.

"Ooh, it's coming down hard," Riley says, huddling close to me under the awning. "Should we make a run for it?"

"Shit." I jab at the release button three more times. "It won't open."

Riley folds her arms over her chest, shifting on her feet. "It's cool. Don't worry about it."

My eyes dart from her warm brown eyes to her twisted locs. "But what about your hair?" I ask, which is apparently a mistake because her upper lip curls as she pins me in place with the return of her favorite expression from hell. "What about my hair?"

"Isn't it sort of a big deal for—"

"For black girls? Ugh. It's obvious you've never dated a black girl. Is that why you brought that janky umbrella?"

I drop my chin and swipe my hand through my wet hair before meeting her gaze again. But this time her expression is soft, alight with...*amusement?*

"Don't laugh, but I might have googled 'things important to black women.'" I let my head fall back and groan. "Shit, that is completely pathetic, isn't it?"

There's a long stretch of silence during which she says nothing, and I feel like a total asshole for having said anything at all.

"I'm totally fucking with you." She giggles. "But your research on my behalf, is maybe the funniest, sweetest...sexiest thing a guy has ever done for me."

All the humor drains from her face and is replaced by a fire so bright, I'm blinded.

In a move I couldn't have come up with in my wildest dreams, Riley steps from underneath the overhang out into the rain letting it drip in streams over her smooth, rich brown skin and through her hair. Under her fixed gaze my pulse quickens as she twists her hands into the drenched fabric of my shirt.

My body comes to attention.

"You got me back for the kiss thing. I call truce." The words claw out of me tortured and gruff. "Please, don't let this be a joke."

Riley erases the distance between us and peeks up at me.

We agreed on sweet smiles and five-second glances, which we'd upped to ten when Spencer James was around. Aside from the framed couple's pictures displayed on both of our desks, that was the extent of our deal.

But, the Lovestruck holiday party is in two weeks, and I know Riley feels the lines blurring too.

The number of walks I've taken past her cubicle alone have tripled—there's only so many cups of coffee I can bring her. I write her silly letters about IT policies and framework, and she responds with hearts and statistics I know she makes up, but I love it. Everything about this fake relationship feels more real than anything I've shared with a woman up to this point.

And, now this.

"Oh, there's *nothing* funny about how I'm feeling right now." A ghost of a smile plays on her lips before she presses them into the curve of my neck electrifying me. The heat of her mouth and the rain sear through me. She's kissing, nipping, tasting, and I haven't even touched her yet.

Every inch of me craves this woman. I'm wrapped up in the scent of her— warm vanilla and coconut—as my muscles lose tension. My breaths come fast and shallow as she gently lifts the brim of my cap and stands up onto her toes. She weaves her hands behind my neck and pins me with a different kind of stare.

This one I love.

"Is this okay?" she asks.

My heart skitters, and I must nod or give some sign of approval because her soft lips brush over mine. With my aching fingers I fist her jacket fabric, tugging her flush to my chest. I pull her lower lip into my mouth, coaxing out the tiniest, sweetest moan. Her breath hitches.

Desire radiates between us, and I deepen the kiss, slipping my tongue between her lips, licking, exploring, matching her rhythm.

She feels so good.

One minute, I'm a bundle of nerves trying not to offend her or overstep her boundaries. The next, this amazing woman is kissing my neck, and her hands are roaming over my chest. My heartbeat revs up. How did we even get here? Is this some part of her plan she failed to let me in on?

But there's no one around to see it...

Every nerve ending on my body stirs and tingles. "Are we really doing this?" I ask, reluctant to hear the answer. Suddenly, someone clears his throat. My eyes snap open. *Her* throat.

"Hey, Jessica..."

Her mouth is hanging open to the wet ground, and her eyes dart between me and Riley, whose wine-colored lipstick is nearly gone.

"Thought you'd left earlier," I say.

"Forgot my phone. Sorry to interrupt." She turns on her hot pink heel, then pauses, twirling her matching umbrella as she pivots back to us with a narrowed gaze. "So, you guys really think you're pulling off this whole—" she gestures her free hand to us "—whatever this sloppy mess is you're doing? Because spoiler alert. You're not. No one believes you've been undercover lovers for four years.

"Oh, right. The 'diamond in the rough' is conveniently in love when Spence is about to announce the new marketing manager."

She gives us a deadpan stare as if it's too much of a bother to match the foam coming from her thin lips with an actual glare.

Riley twists in my arms, but she doesn't move to step away. Her stare travels slowly from Jessica's heels up to her eyes before she speaks. "Are you mad? Jealous?" she asks evenly.

Jessica huffs. "Of what?"

"Let's see. I've been here three and a half years, and you've been here five, yet we're in the same position. You've likely had to do unthinkable things to get in good with Eric Voorhees who, the word on the street is, didn't quit but got fired. And Spencer still doesn't know who you are...no matter how many muffins and coffees you bring him."

Whoa. Shit.

Jessica taps her toe, sending a light spray dancing in the air.

"And this?" Riley leans her back against my chest, wrapping my arm over her shoulder and down to her waist so that my hand rests on her stomach. "Spencer already knows about us. In fact, he sounded pretty excited when he personally invited us to come to the holiday party together. So, whatever *you're* thinking…don't. I would tell you to go about your business, but sadly, it seems you have none."

As soon as Jessica stalks off like someone just stole her bike, I pick up where we left off.

"I'm not assuming anything, but if you decide you want to take this thing to the next level, I want you to talk to me just like you did Jessica." I laugh and flatten my hand on Riley's stomach. "You can wear one of those naughty Mrs. Claus outfits…or, just a bow. And get a reindeer whip."

If we're blurring lines, might as well erase them.

Then Riley turns back to me.

The confident woman who just checked Jessica and put her in her place is gone. Riley's eyes are wide and round. She's paralyzed with fear. "Shit. Oh, shit. We're totally going to get caught lying. Spencer's going to fire us. We'll be blackballed. I never should have—"

"It'll be fine."

"I'm sorry I got you involved. We have to end this *now*."

CHAPTER FIVE

I t's been two days since "the kiss."

That's what I call it when Nina and I talk about it—followed by my immediate cringe. It's not that Chase Campbell isn't a ridiculously beautiful male specimen, but what was I thinking going rogue and snapping at Jessica? What possessed me to put my lips on his neck? On his lips? Why was I mentally calculating the logistics of climbing him like Mount Everest?

Flashes of Chase growling between kisses flood back to me. His hand tangled in my hair as we'd explored each other's hungry mouths. How hard he'd been for me. Desire flickers back to life in my body, which throbs for him.

Temporary insanity.

Stress.

That's the only way to explain it—a lapse in judgment brought on by the whole fantastical scene. How many romcoms have I watched and given the requisite swoon when the rain kiss flashes across the screen? Obviously, too many to count. As soon as I got my opportunity to star in one, I snatched it up really quick.

I technically called it off with Chase two days ago, but have I spilled the beans to Spencer? No.

Ugh. What am I doing? What am I waiting for?

I stretch my neck to peek over the top of my cubicle and immediately slump back down in my chair. *Shit.* He saw me.

For probably the fifth time today.

"This is a place of business," Nina says from her desk directly across from mine. Her tone is dripping with sarcasm as she stabs at her keyboard. "I can't concentrate with all this sexual tension."

Me, either.

But also, exactly.

This *is* a place of business. Which is why I'm staying at my desk like a good girl. Why I redrew the blurred line in bold permanent ink is beyond me. This is a *fake* relationship, not some cutesy holiday office romance. There's not supposed to be sex. *Or, kissing.*

No matter how much I want to lick him like ice cream.

I clear my throat and sit up taller, determined to be productive if it kills me. "Can you keep it down over there? Some of us are trying to work." *And failing miserably.*

Nina peeks over the top of her cubicle toward Chase's desk and shakes her head like we're both too exhausting to deal with.

Don't look at him.

This is why everything is so confusing now—Frankly, I don't know what possessed me to put my lips on his wet, hot skin. It's been a while since I dated anyone, but I didn't even think I was attracted to white boys. I mean, has he even dated a black girl before? *Ugh, why does that even matter? None of this is real.* But after he said he'd Googled for me, and the way he looked at me like he wanted to take me up against the wall right there on the side of the building…

The worst part is, as horny as I am, I would've let him.

"Is that why it's almost lunch and you've done nothing but stare at him from your desk?" Nina asks. "Sitting there all hot and bothered…skin all flushed… Breathe."

I don't even have to turn to know she's reclined her chair all the way back and is staring at me with the same smug smile from this morning when Chase and I exchanged an awkward hug.

You'd think I'd have told Spencer this relationship isn't real but nope. Still dragging out the ruse.

"Riley, in all the time we've worked together, you have never taken off your blazer. The man has driven you to show your shoulders, for goodness sake. Either go talk to him or meet me in the lunchroom." Nina says.

The woman is crazy. And making no sense. I have so taken off my jacket. *I think.*

"For what?"

She doesn't validate my question with an answer. Cool as a cucumber, she stands and sashays out of her cubicle toward the lunchroom without so much as a side glance my way.

"Okay…" I heave a sigh, prop my elbows on my desk, and promptly begin massaging my temples.

My unfinished proposal for additional security features and a choose-your-own pricing-and-match model stares back at me from my screen. I have less than two weeks to finish it along with all my other accounts. I should be buckling down to knock this out so I can enjoy the holiday season.

My stomach gurgles.

Fuck it.

Greatness will not be achieved if I'm starving. I lock my screen, grab my purse, and push back from the desk, taking long, hurried strides to meet Nina. When I reach the lunchroom, I collide with the familiar wall of muscles attached to the man who's been starring in my "me time" for the past couple of nights.

Heat crawls from my neck to my cheeks, and my heart gives a little lurch. "Hey…"

"Riley." A pink blush grows on his adorable face. His lips part slightly like he wants to say more—or do more. "Thanks for coming."

I feel my eyebrows crease, but then Nina pops her head into the doorframe, and I know Chase and I have been set up.

"Told you. Sexual tension."

As she moseys down the hall, I hear her singing "All I Want for Christmas is You." I remind myself to pay her back for this later.

And thank her.

"Listen, I know you said you wanted to dial it back a bit, but I was wondering if you'd like to grab some food with me?" Chase asks. "There's a little Mexican place not too far from here near Town Center. We can sit and talk."

A better woman would tell Chase no and keep things simple—smiles and exchanging silly letters. Maybe I should give my career more than a passing thought, considering I might get blackballed when we get caught lying.

I'm not a better woman.

At this moment, with this man looking at me like I'm the reason he breathes, I'm just a woman who would risk everything to see if any part of what I'm feeling could be real.

ROSITA'S IS ONE OF THOSE ASSEMBLY LINE RESTAURANTS WHERE WE customize our burritos, tacos, or salad bowls—black beans or refried beans, carne or pollo, extra guac, hold the pico de gallo. None of which I care about at the moment. How can I eat when my heart is in my throat?

We're on our third or fourth closed-end question when I flatten my hands on the table.

"Listen, Riley. I don't want things to be awkward between us. I asked you to lunch so we can talk."

"Yeah, no worries." She shrugs, but the tension in her shoulders doesn't ease up, so I know she's in the same place I am.

"Feliz Navidad" is playing in the background, and the upbeat rhythm is in direct contrast with my current mood.

"But I am worried because...I like you." Her eyes snap to mine and my pulse revs up. "I get it. This was supposed to be a ploy so Spencer would give you real consideration for the promotion without focusing on your personal life, but... Tell me you didn't feel something Tuesday night in the rain, and I'll drop this right now," I blurt out.

Riley swallows, but her lips are parted.

I can almost hear her heartbeat—a heavy thump jackhammering against her chest to the same rhythm as mine. It's always the same when something is on the line.

"The thing is—" she begins.

"Wait." The thought of Riley telling me she didn't feel the magnetic field forcing our bodies together and synchronizing our heartbeats is disheartening.

Leaning forward, I slide my hands over the table to take hers in mine. With a little squeeze, I search her eyes. Her brown irises are hard with the same apprehension I feel.

"Before you say anything, I'm not asking you to make this official or to be with me—just yet." The corners of her mouth gently tug upward. "We sort of bypassed all the 'getting to know you' stuff and ended up with our lips attached. Which was amazing, by the way, but I know it's a little much. All I'm asking is if we can take a couple of steps back. I want to know you. I want you to know me. And if you like what you learn, then maybe we can see what's here."

I hate that I feel like I'm begging, but everything about this moment, the alarm ringing in my mind, the way my stomach knots, the fear twisting my gut, makes it impossible to pretend this is nothing and continue wondering what would have happened. Everything about this moment feels urgent.

She doesn't say anything for a few seconds, and I don't rush her. If she decides to give us a try, it has to be on her terms.

"Okay. What's your favorite Christmas movie?" she asks straight-faced, and I chuckle. I can't deny the hope fluttering inside me. "This all started because of a holiday party, so let's start there and work our way around to more serious stuff."

Okay. That's not a no...

"Some people won't count it. It's an unpopular opinion, but it is technically Christmastime in the movie..." I stretch my hands to hers, twining our fingers, which is quickly starting to feel like a habit.

Her delicate hands are warm and soft. The rich brown hue gives off a glow. When held against my complexion, the contrast is even more stark. They fit so seamlessly in my grasp, though, it's a perfect reflection of us. We're yin and yang—opposites in every way, connecting to make a whole. Complementary.

"Don't laugh, but…it's *Gremlins*," I admit, bracing myself for the usual backlash I get when people hear my favorite is anything other than a classic.

When Riley gasps, my eyes dart from our hands to her wide eyes.

Her mouth is wide open. "Shut up."

"Gizmo is a Christmas gift. It counts."

"No. I know. It's just… *Gremlins* is *my* favorite Christmas movie. My whole family makes fun of me because it's not *This Christmas* or *Elf* or *Miracle on 34th Street*. At least with *Gremlins*, there's no 'happy tears.'"

"Couldn't agree more." I lift my chin smugly. "See? We already have something in common."

She shakes her head in disbelief. "Let's try again. What song? And you have to be specific about the rendition and the singer."

"Easy. 'All I Want for Christmas Is You.' Mariah Carey." I pull my lower lip between my teeth and wait for it.

"Same. But that's everyone's favorite." She releases her right hand and stacks her fork with beans, cheesy rice, chicken, and lettuce before shoveling it in her mouth. "What about drinks?" she asks over another mouthful.

I don't go for the dealbreaker right off the bat. "Don't tell me you're a PSL girl."

She looks confused. "Why do I feel like I should be offended?"

"Pumpkin spice latte. If you didn't immediately know what it was, it's safe to say you're good."

"Actually, I'm more of a PML, Peppermint Mocha Latte, girl if we're being specific. It's like a Christmas mistletoe in a cup. Then again, anything's better than the crappy lunchroom coffee."

If Riley wasn't convinced we've got something that could work, fifteen minutes later, we agree eggnog is the worst beverage ever (holiday or not), Christmas gumdrop nougat is the best candy, and, even though the colors mean nothing, the red and green M&M cookies are the best. If we add in the fact both of us always wait until the last minute to do our gift shopping, there's no denying we're a Christmas romance made in heaven at the very least.

When she relaxes, my whole mood lifts. My appetite returns, but we're out of time, so I'll have to eat at my desk. We head back, and I park the car feeling buoyed with a fresh energy as I take Riley's hand with my right and the to-go bag in my left.

We walk toward the Lovestruck building in a comfortable silence.

Every second her hand is in mine, I'm more certain of this easiness and the innocence of just being together. It's something my parents shared in their relationship. It's not the whole of it, but it's definitely a key ingredient in what makes up real love.

CHAPTER SIX

Sometime between lunch yesterday and *Good Morning Las Vegas* blaring on my television this morning, something got screwed up. And by *something*, I mean me.

I mean, Chase and I left off on such a good note. He said he had *feelings* for me, which, let's face it, melted my heart. It felt like maybe we'd see what could happen between us, but then all the best-case scenarios eventually bled into the worst. Now, I can't get it out of my head that building a new relationship based on a lie isn't the best place to start.

I didn't plan on real...

While I throw on a simple black pantsuit and twist my locs up into an easy bun, I keep tossing around what course of action to take—I can't *not* do anything. It's Friday, and I won't make it through the weekend with this on my chest. It's now or never. Either I tell Spencer this whole relationship with Chase has been a lie and risk losing him or keep up the charade and never know if we could've had something.

After applying blush and mascara, I lock up and hop in my car with my stomach tied up in knots. Knowing what I have to do weighs on me. My integrity is at stake here. No matter what my heart is telling me, I have to come clean to Spencer now even if it means sabotaging my career—and my only chance with Chase.

As I veer into the road, I flip on the radio.

Mistletoe memories of just us two. Baby, no matter the season, I love you.

Turning up the volume, I let my favorite singer, Bianca, drown out my worries. I crack my neck, singing along as I ease off the gas, pulling to a stop at a red light just as my phone rings on Bluetooth, cutting off my jam.

"Hey, Ke," I say to my little sister, Keira. "What's going on?"

"Morning. Just checking in to see whether you're going to the parental units' on Christmas Eve or the actual day," she says, sounding way too cheery for...7:50.

Damn. No time to stop for good coffee.

I crack my neck and sigh out my frustrations about the coffee. I'm ready for the holiday. I could use more jingle bells and white elephants in my life right now. "Probably Christmas Eve. You know I like to be lazy and watch movies on the day. Why? What were you thinking?"

"Well..."

She trails off, and immediately my shoulders tense. That breathy purr coupled with the fact she's up before noon can only mean one thing.

"I met a guy!" She squeals into the line like she can barely keep it together long enough to get it out. "Oh my gosh. Riley, when I tell you he is fine, I mean, he is *fine*." When she says it, it sounds more like *foin*. "He's tall—like basketball player tall—but not scrawny with full lips, hair faded up, and rich, dark skin. He sounds even better than he looks—I mean, from what I can tell. We haven't actually met in person yet."

I take a deep breath because I want to be happy for her. I really do, but I've read so many studies about the risks of modern dating. Reports of rape linked to online dating increase exponentially each year. It's not just women required to take so many extra precautions in their search for a soul mate, either. It's exhausting, and frankly, scary.

"So…"

"And before you even ask how I met him, don't. You have got to stop worrying about me and that one time, years ago. I'm okay, and I'm meeting him during the day. It'll be out in the open, with a bunch of people around. I'll be completely safe."

That gives me zero comfort.

A billion safety questions pop into my head. Who are you keeping in the loop with all his info and the date plans? Are you driving your own car? How much are you planning to drink? If you do, will you remember not more than two and not to leave your drink unattended? Is there anyone else around for a group date? How about the mace and the pepper spray I gave you? At the very, very least, have you googled him? I know all of that will definitely make her shut down, so I start with the least ominous query.

"Which app was it?" I ask, aiming for breezy, but it comes out overbearing. As usual.

In typical Keira form, she heaves a loud sigh. "*See?* Ugh. I shouldn't have even brought it up. This is why I didn't want to tell you—"

"I'm sorry. I promise, I'm happy for you. You know, I just worry. "

She sucks her teeth loudly into the line. "Whatever. The point is, I'll be at Mom and Dad's on Christmas Eve, too. For our first date, Thomas and I are going to the Snowball Jam at the T-Mobile Arena on the holiday."

"Dang. You got tickets?" I ask, genuinely jealous.

"Yep, and you know Bianca is headlining."

For a few minutes, I let my sister rub it in my face before I remember all the possible dangers of being at a huge arena with a guy she doesn't know from Adam.

After I beg her to at least take the lipstick-shaped taser I bought for her last birthday—and because I feel guilty as hell for hovercoptering her—I spend the last three minutes of my drive giving her the CliffsNotes version of my current cluster-fuck of a career and phony relationship.

By the time I pull into my usual space outside the Lovestruck building, I'm out of breath, and still not all the way awake. *I need coffee in the worst way.* "So, anyway, I'm basically screwed, but I can't let Chase take the fall for me."

Naturally, the first question out of her mouth is "Did you kiss him?"

Freaking hopeless romantic.

Why did I open this can of worms? I dart my eyes to the clock on the dashboard. At this point, if there's any chance of salvaging my job, on top of lying to my boss, lateness is probably not going to help my case.

"Yes, but I don't have time to get into the details," I say, tapping the speakerphone widget and cutting the engine, but it's too late. Keira is already geeked up for her chance to harass me about a guy. "Relax. Did you not hear me say 'fake relationship?' He's just playing the part."

I feel a tiny pang in my heart saying this given how Chase laid his feelings out on the table for me yesterday.

"Uh-uh. Riley, you kissed in the rain and cussed out a coworker. If anything is fake, it's this little act you're putting on for me. You *like* him. Is he *foin?*"

She can't see me, but I roll my eyes because I. Do. Not. Have. Time. For. This. "See? Ugh. This is why I didn't want to tell you anything," I say, taking a cue from her book. "I have more important things to worry about right now." *Like my job.*

I punch my code into the keypad and quietly shuffle down the hall toward the cubicle maze, stopping short of Spencer's office. Keira's still arguing her points—plural—as I peek around the corner through the glass.

Thank the lord, heaven, and stars, he's not in yet.

A wave of relief washes over me, and I blow out a breath

despite Keira's relentless attempt to help me out of my own way in the dating department.

I'm a professional.

"The way I see it, he's like the fiery ginger stallion to your fierce ice queen. And with *Gremlins* and the cookies and shit? It's a freaking Christmas miracle match made in heaven. Please, I'm begging you not to be a Scrooge Grinch for once and give this dude a chance."

"I'm about to hang up on—"

"All I'm saying is talk to Chase. See how you feel about him today and if the spark is still there. If not, fine. Go throw yourself under the bus on Monday. If your boss fires you, take the whole week off."

As I walk out into the open every pair of eyes in the building snap to me. I freeze in place, flitting a glance to Nina whose unblinking brown ones are wide and round as she slowly stands and starts shuffling toward me.

Shit.

"Ke. I gotta go."

"No one does crazy stuff on Fridays. I'm telling you, you'll be worried all weekend—" she's saying as I end the call, cutting her off. I jam the phone into my blazer pocket and brace myself.

When Nina reaches me, she practically shoves me into the lunchroom. The tight smile she flashes Darrell and Charlotte who are lingering near the crap coffee scares them off pretty quickly. Finally, we're alone.

"What happened?" I ask.

"Are you kidding me? Apparently, Spencer James flew out to the San Diego office last night for some big division meeting. He's gone until Monday."

So much for coming clean to Spencer and accepting my ticket to the unemployment line.

Okay, so how does *his* weekend meeting relate to *me*?

My shoulders are up to my ears and my eyebrows are up to my hairline. *Tell me why I should care.*

"Let's just say, when the cat's away…" Nina crosses her arms over her chest and pierces me with a pointed stare. "Your girl, Jessica, has been running off at the mouth telling anyone who'll listen—which basically means everyone—that Chase had you pinned against the side of the building in the rain Tuesday night. Kissing, rubbing, practically *loving*." She wiggles her brows.

I close my eyes and pinch the bridge of my nose. "What did he say?"

"Holy shit. It's true. You guys totally hooked up—"

"We kissed. That was all…before I came to my senses. I was actually planning to talk to Spencer today to clear this all up, but I guess I'll have to wait until Monday."

Nina's mouth falls open. "Nope. Don't even try it. I saw how smitten you were after the whole lunch setup. You totally like him."

"Oh my gosh. First Keira, now you? I'm too through with you guys. If you…" I break out into laughter, walking away, and raise my volume loud enough for the entire building to hear. "…or if anyone else who needs to get a life wants to know where I am, I'll be minding my business listening to glorious Christmas songs on repeat at my desk."

When I step into my cubicle, there's coffee on my desk. Not the crappy lunchroom stuff. It's the familiar blue and yellow cup from my favorite café with a neon green Post-it stuck to it.

I let my purse slide down my arm onto my chair and inch close enough to read the shorthand "pepp moch latte" on the cup. I pull my bottom lip between my teeth and pick up the note.

Riley, I like you a latte. Meet you under the mistletoe.

Chase

As much as I try, I can't bite back the shit-eating grin on my face.

"What was that you were saying?"

I peek over at Nina whose expression is one of smug delight. She knew this was waiting for me all along. I was supposed to tell Spencer everything today, but he isn't here. Unfortunately, or fortunately—I haven't decided which—Chase is.

———————

THE DAY DRAGS BY AT A GLACIAL PACE TO THE TUNE OF A WINTRY wonderland soundtrack. If I have to hear "All I Want for Christmas" one more time, I'm going to gauge my eardrums out with a fucking candy cane.

I get it, Spencer's out of town, and everyone's reveling in the holiday spirit and making plans for the weekend, but I'm not exactly in the mood. Yesterday, Riley and I had an amazing time at lunch. I brought her favorite coffee this morning and not a word. Since I haven't been able to catch her alone, it's self-quarantine at my desk.

To make matters worse, not only haven't I been able to talk to Riley, but Jessica Faulkner decided to strike while the iron's hot and tell everyone Riley and I are in the middle of a "lover's quarrel."

Give me a break.

Even with my headphones on, I pretend not to hear them talking or see them staring, but I guess the noise-canceling feature on these things isn't the best.

"Dang, you got Renee? I'm stuck with Craig," Darrell says to someone. His deep baritone climbs over the walls of my cubicle. "What's the gift limit again?"

Not that I was intently listening, but I miss the answer as they walk away. My phone pings beside my computer.

Todd 4:59 pm
If you ever come up for air, let's grab some beers at the bar next
Sunday for the game.

Come up for air? Even my brother knows I'm drowning.

My eyes dart to the scrap of paper I crumpled up and pushed aside near the framed picture of Riley and me. I've never once participated in the Secret Santa gift exchange everyone does every year.

So why isn't the paper in the trash bin?

I groan, just as Nina pops her head over the top of the wall. "Hey, lover boy," she teases.

"Hey, Nina. How's it going?" I sit up taller and swivel to face her.

"Better than you two sexually frustrated stubborn asses." She laughs and darts her eyes to my desk before slowly snapping them back to me. "I see you're both trying to flake out on Darrell's Secret Santa party Saturday night."

I flit a glance over to the wrinkled paper with Riley's name on it. "Yeah. I'm probably just going to lay low this weekend and maybe get some Christmas shopping done," I say, knowing good and well I've never purchased a gift before December twenty-fourth.

Then, I notice the music is off. It's quiet. Nina is walking away.

"Where are you going?" I ask.

"Home, like normal people do at five o'clock," she calls over her shoulder. "It's just you guys still burning the midnight oil."

Right on cue, someone hits the overhead lights and the building goes dark except for the light from my cubicle…and the one directly across from where Nina sits. Nina is busily digging in her purse. I flip my wrist to check the time. There's no way it's…

When did it get so late?

"Damn, I must've gotten caught up in this app update." I recline in my chair clasping my fingers behind my head. "Guess it's time to pack it in."

"That's what she said…" Nina replies and waggles her brows. "I mean, if you guys decide to stay here all weekend, you can always do it on the conference table."

Not that I wouldn't mind living out fantasies with Riley, but I'm pretty sure she's gotta speak to me first.

"Bye, Nina." I wave her off as she backs away with an expression that can only be read as "make it happen."

After I slip on my jacket, gather my things, and flip off the light, I take slow deliberate strides toward Riley's desk. "Hey. Want some company walking out to your car?" I ask.

My voice startles her and she jerks back against her chair with her hand pressed to her chest. "Shoot! Chase. Hey."

"Sorry. I didn't mean to scare you, it's just everyone's already gone, and I didn't want you to walk out by yourself."

"Oh, don't worry about it. Nina just left a few minutes ago. I can probably still catch up to her if you have plans or something." She swallows, and her tongue dips out to lick her lips. She's breathless and breathtaking.

I can't move.

We're both frozen in the moment waiting for this to be less awkward. I've been pretty clear that I want her. After lunch, I thought she might be getting there, too. Then she went silent on me, so now I don't know. Except, I see the heat in her hooded eyes, the rapid rise and fall of her chest, and the way she's gripping the chair like she needs something to hold onto... She feels something. She looks...*stricken?*

Is she afraid?

She almost looks fragile.

Then something hits me like a lightning bolt. *The app features.* That day Spencer announced the marketing manager vacancy, she mentioned wanting to make it safe for women. *Did something happen to her?*

My throat feels tight. "Do you want me to leave?" I ask just in case I've misread everything, disregarded her boundaries when she's saying no and I'm only thinking about what I want.

We're a woman and a man alone at night with no one else around. Even her sitting and me standing, it's a power shift. It's off-putting, but somehow, I get the feeling it has nothing to do with me.

Instinctively, I take a step back.

Riley straightens like I've just given her the space to breathe. The tension in her shoulders drains slightly at my question. "I'm sorry. No." She shakes her head like she's knocking loose a thought, refocusing her surroundings. "No, I don't want you to leave. You sorta caught me off guard, that's all."

This side of Riley is new to me. She's always so buttoned-up—the tunnel-vision businessperson with her eyes focused on the ball, willing to do whatever she must to realize her goals. This side of her is so firmly on defense. But, against what or who? I don't know how to reconcile the tentative posture and tight expression with the take-charge woman who kissed me in the rain.

"Do you have much more you need to do before you're ready to leave?"

"No. I was about to log off anyway." She starts tapping away at the keyboard, closing out windows, and clearing her calendar before she grabs her purse and keys.

For a second, I'm standing there drumming my fingers on the top of the cubicle wall, weighing how much to say when I notice the shape of her wine-stained lips on the brim of the coffee cup I bought this morning.

"Are you hungry? Maybe we can get a bite and you can tell me what happened today..."

Riley blinks up at me.

Her shoulders curve in slightly. "Pizza?" She flashes me a hopeful smile and I nod.

"Where'd you have in mind?"

She gets her coat on, flips the light switch, and now she's at my side as we walk toward the exit. "Would you be okay if we ordered in?" Her smile is soft, coy, and her eyes sparkle with newfound amusement.

I toss her a surprised look then decide not to press my good luck.

"Okay. Your place or mine?"

Riley pulls her bottom lip between her teeth. "Do you have Flixshow? They just released the live action *Final Tombs* movie. We can talk between zombie attacks."

"Isn't that based on the video game? You're a gamer?" I ask, failing to contain the shock in my tone.

A brush of cool air washes over us as we step outside. Our cars are the only two in the lot, but we're not parked too far apart.

"Don't sound so amazed. There's a lot you don't know about me, Chase Campbell." *So much I want to know.* Riley bumps my shoulder and starts backing away toward her car. "Oh, before I forget, I don't know if you heard Jessica telling everyone we're having a 'lover's quarrel.'" She laughs then gives me a half-shrug, shaking her head. "Well, Nina shut her down and told her we'd be at Darrell's Secret Santa thing tomorrow night."

"Okay," I say, even though seeing my coworkers outside of work sounds like hell.

Riley fishes her keys out from her purse and jingles them in the air. "I hope you didn't get Craig." She laughs, rolling her eyes. "Text me your address in case I lose you."

You won't.

CHAPTER SEVEN

"Thirty minutes or the pizza's free," Chase looks up from his phone.

Why did I come here?

Somewhere in the back of my mind, I thought being in his space, learning more about the good man he is, would reaffirm my decision to call it quits. No one wants to see the good guy go down as collateral damage. But after being here and seeing his neat little place with his tiny Christmas tree and pictures of his family lining his bookshelves, my plan has backfired.

I'm sitting ramrod straight on the edge of his couch with my heart in my throat.

When I blink out of my daze, he's staring at me and looking totally ravishing. He narrows his gaze, and I make the mistake of letting my eyes drift to his lips. Now all I can think about is how he tasted like mint and warm coffee.

I tug at the collar of my coat. "Do you have anything to drink?"

Chase flashes me a questioning smile as he shoves his phone in his back pocket and walks over to the fridge, ducking his head inside. "Yeah, I just went to the supermarket last night. Let's see, I've got water, beer, wine, and an array of berry-flavored juices…" He peeks up over the refrigerator door with his big adorable eyes.

Why am I doing this to myself? And why can't I stop thinking about the roughness of his beard on my lips…and on my thighs?

Stop.

"Hmm. Let me take a look." I pad over and peek inside, but the red and green packaging of a certain favorite holiday candy snags my attention. "Is that…"

"Oh."

"No, no. Did you go out and *buy* the ingredients for the M&M Christmas cookies and a bag of the peppermint nougat?" I cannot close my mouth.

He's not going to make this easy.

Chase lowers his chin, but he can't hide his smile.

"You are so busted. Did you plan this? Were you secretly luring me here to your house, acting all sweet and innocent?" I tip up his chin, so he has to look at me. "You are *not* sweet and innocent Chase Campbell."

We're both laughing as he pulls out the ingredients and stacks them on the kitchen counter. The pizza will be here in like twenty minutes, but now that I know there are Christmas treats, what kind of person doesn't drop everything to make them?

"The baking sheets are in that bottom drawer beneath the oven." He gives me a sexy wink, and I feel my willpower waning.

I don't stand a chance against those guilty, sexy eyes with that rough and tumble beard. "What should I set the oven to?"

It takes us less than five minutes to get the mixing bowls, oil spray, and aluminum foil all lined up. Seamlessly, we move around each other in comfortable silence. Chase lines the baking sheets while I pour the M&Ms into the bowl with ready-made sugar cookie dough. I spray, he kneads—and boy does he do it well.

The hard muscles of his forearms flex and bulge. He does this ridiculously sexy lip-biting thing. "So, I wanted to ask you something," he says, using his strong fingers to work the dough.

"Yeah?"

He hands me an ice cream scoop and I start spacing out the cookie balls on the baking sheet.

"Back there at the office when we were leaving, you seemed a little—"

"I know. I'm so sorry. It really wasn't about you," I say, knowing it's probably too much to ask for him to drop the subject.

He nods, and he's kind enough not to say anything, but the questions in his silence blare too loud.

"Two years ago, my younger sister..." I start, but the words die off.

"You don't have to tell me if you don't want to. It's just, you seemed almost guarded like you were afraid. I never want to make anyone feel that way."

A few seconds go by. Chase doesn't force the conversation, but there's something so unassuming about his tone and his sweet concern. I want to tell him and lift the weight from my chest.

"She went on a date with some guy she met on one of those low-key, sketchy match sites—it got shut down a few months later, but at the time it had been popular. Like we've seen too many times at work, of course, he didn't look anything like the picture. Go figure." I fish a leftover green M&M from the bag and pop it in my mouth. "Anyway, she decided to give him a chance and stay for the date because they had really good rapport online, you know?"

"Right."

The oven beeps indicating the oven is the right temperature. Chase quickly washes and dries his hands. "I'm listening," he says as he slides the cookie sheet into the oven and sets the timer.

"Long story short, in person, the conversation ended up being just as shitty as his fake picture. So, she excused herself to the restroom to call me, right? But while I'm on the phone with her, he enters the women's restroom and proceeds to force himself on her while I'm freaking out on the phone."

Chase's shoulders tense as he pivots to me, searching my eyes, but he doesn't interrupt. We're both leaning against the edge of the sink facing each other.

"Luckily, another woman came in behind him, which distracted him long enough for my sister to knee him in his junk and escape. But all I ever think about is what if that woman hadn't showed up? What if he'd had his way with her?"

My throat clenches at the thought. It still feels like a knife to my heart. My sister was assaulted, and I was helpless to do anything. The same fear flares in my gut leaving me raw with emotion.

With a warm and welcoming smile, Chase opens his arms. "Bring it in."

I laugh through my tears.

It's such a strange sensation because I don't hesitate or come up with a million reasons why not to. I sink into his embrace, resting my cheek to his hard chest. I'm wrapped in his clean, warm scent, and it feels better than I remembered. We don't say anything, we just stand there with his arms banded around me.

He peppers soft kisses in my hair slowly lulling the wretched memory back to the dark corners of my mind.

When my tears subside, the urge to explain overwhelms me.

"She's why I'm at Lovestruck," I explain. "It's not just women either, everyone is vulnerable. It's why I want to introduce more safety features on the app, whether it's enabling location, adding distress alarms, or even a button to notify emergency contacts. We have to be purposeful about the real dangers people face when they meet up. We can't possibly know everything there is to know about our users."

I pull back from his embrace and register the empathy in his beautiful blue eyes. "I get it," he whispers sweetly, but it's his heated stare that electrifies me.

His gaze drifts from my eyes to my lips, lingering for a dizzying beat. Desire radiates between us sending heat curling down my spine. My breath catches.

Then the doorbell rings, saving me from myself.

He closes his eyes for a second, letting his shoulders sag at his sides. "Hold that thought. Pizza's here."

As Chase takes wide strides to the front door and digs his hand in his back pocket for his wallet, I blow out a relieved sigh. I bury my face in my hands. My heart pounds against my chest because I know I'm fighting a losing battle. Now that I know Chase isn't a player, my reservations are more about him getting hurt in the fallout if Spencer ever learns the truth about us. Also, I shouldn't like him as much as I do.

If I had any sense, I'd leave now.

———

WE'RE BOTH TWO SLICES IN WHEN RILEY PLOPS BACK ON THE COUCH and sighs. "I'm full." She laughs and groans. "I should've gone home first and changed my clothes because these pants and Italian food don't mix."

"So, what I'm hearing you say is, no Christmas cookies for you." I flash her a playful grin. I love this easy banter, but I wish we could go back to the moment right before the doorbell rang.

Something changed...shifted. For a few minutes, I got to see behind her carefully constructed walls. She let me in.

Riley sucks her teeth, slouching into the crease of the couch. "Oh, I may have to lose a button, but I will not be passing up on dessert."

On the television, sharp piercing music plays as the zombies of *Final Tombs* close in on the heroine. Riley is curled up behind a throw pillow she's been using to shield her eyes, but she just looks so uncomfortable.

I take a bite out of another slice and stand to take her empty plate, flashing her a quick smile. "Want some sweats and a t-shirt?" I ask as I walk away into the kitchen.

Shit.

It's just a simple gesture, but immediately I wonder if I shouldn't have offered. After everything she told me about her sister, I don't want to assume anything.

Riley doesn't answer right away. It's silent save for the heavy breathing of zombies, but then she surprises me when she says, "Sure."

I glance over at her and there's apprehension and questions in her eyes I'm not sure I can answer. How did we get here? Are we really doing this? Is any of it real? I want to tell her I've been here all along waiting for her to notice me, that I take the long way around to my desk just to see her eyes, and how beautiful I think she is no matter how she wears her hair or which black suit she chooses.

Instead, I fill a plate with cookies, set them on the coffee table, and go to grab clothes for her, eager to put some space between us so I can think straight.

A few minutes later, Riley questions me from the bathroom while she changes. "So, what's your story Chase? What are you doing at Lovestruck?" Riley asks. "Web development and IT are like the most sought-after fields."

Pointing the remote at the television, I lower the volume so I can hear her. "It's a good gig. Pays well... Also, I get to leave work at work."

The bathroom door creaks open and Riley walks out, drowning in my clothes. *Fuck.* The way the fabric hangs off her lean curves, breasts, and her ass... My dick twitches.

"Better?"

"Oh my gosh, yes. I can breathe." She's glowing and radiant as she gives me a twirl before plopping down next to me on the couch. "About the job, if those are your reasons, you're obviously not challenging yourself. I mean, what drives you every day?"

She twists to face me, curling her knees to her chest, but she doesn't speak. She's waiting for me to fill in the unspoken blanks.

"Fine." I close my eyes and let my head rest on the back of the couch. "It's nothing as horrific as what your sister went through, but, don't laugh... I wanted to be in an environment where I could learn about love."

I peek over at Riley. Her brows furrow, but her expression is more curious than anything.

"My parents were married forty years before my mom died of

pneumonia—complications with cystic fibrosis. My brother, Todd, seems to have found his person, and I mean, I've dated, but it always feels superficial, slightly like an interview." I laugh. "This is going to sound really cliché, but I want to know about "the real thing." Lovestruck just felt like a place close to home to find some insight."

When Riley doesn't immediately say anything, I tilt my head to the side again to look at her. She bites her lower lip, and her eyes are misted over.

"There's nothing cliché about anything you just said. It's beautiful."

Then, Riley lowers her legs, crawls over to me, and straddles me. My breath hitches at the feel of her. Silence stretches between us for a beat before I slowly, carefully, sit upright. Our faces are a breath apart as she levels me with a pleading stare. I know she needs to make the first move, so I wait.

Desperately.

My skin tingles. Every inch of my body throbs and aches with the need to feel her touch.

Please let this be real.

My heart knocks around in my chest. The anticipation is killing me. I don't mind handing over the reins as long as it's Riley who's wielding them.

"Put your hands on me, Chase." Her breaths come fast and shallow, and I feel her fighting it.

I slide my hands under ass, centering her over the hard proof of how much she turns me on. Even though she feels like a dream, everything about this moment is real. She's flush against my chest, and still I wait. "Tell me what you want," I whisper.

"I want you to kiss me," she says, and I feel so privileged that she wants me, too.

I comply slowly. The kiss is sensual and sweeping with, exploring tongues and roaming hands. There's a sweetness and lightness that sends warmth surging through me. I like Riley, but I could so easily love her.

We're being so careful with each other's hearts. We're mindful of every amazing nip and painstakingly slow lick.

My pulse quickens as desire percolates between us. I'm lost in her warm vanilla scent. A growl pries its way out of me.

She moans and I tighten my grip on her ass in response.

"I want this," she says between kisses. Her tone is low, breathy, and almost sheepish, like she's saying it to herself.

I scoot to the edge of the couch and stand upright holding her, "Are you sure about this?"

Her answering kiss is all the permission I need. In quick strides, I carry her with her body molded to mine to my room and lay her onto the bed. The blankets shroud around her as I slowly glide the sweatpants off her one leg at a time before lifting the T-shirt up over her head. The sight of her bright-red bra and panties set coaxes a growl from me. Every inch of her rich, dark skin is smooth and flawless and begging to be touched.

My breath catches at the masterpiece of feminine curves and shadows. "You're so fucking beautiful."

Heat pools in her hooded eyes.

As if the sight of her pliant body lying in my bed wasn't enough, she dips a finger in her mouth and begins sucking it as she tugs at the waistband of her panties, slowly dragging them over her hips.

I step backward to get a condom from my nightstand, too afraid if I turn away, she'll be gone when I look back. It feels like a dream to have Riley in my bed. I'm blindsided with lust as I remove my shirt and pants, aching to be inside her.

As she shimmies free from her panties and lets her knees hang open, I have to hold my breath not to come. My breaths come fast and shallow as I kick off my boxers and roll on the condom in supersonic speed.

A ghost of a smile plays on her lips.

"Don't make me laugh right now," I say. "If I even sneeze, I'm going to come."

The sweet, musical laugh Riley lets out echoes off the walls.

"We wouldn't want that now, would we?" She's biting back a grin and my heart skitters.

I close my eyes. "Just be cool. Just let me think about football or polar bears or something."

Riley doesn't hold back this time, she's bent over with laughter. "Come here, you fool."

"Please stop laughing. Do you have any idea how sexy your laugh is?" I feel her warm laugh all over my skin. "Not to mention, this is sort of embarrassing."

The next thing I know Riley's yanking me down on top of her, planting kisses all over my face. She reaches between us and encircles her hand around me, stroking for a few seconds before centering me against her sex.

As I grip her hips and bury myself inside her, her slick folds open around me, and every sensation in my body heightens. A shiver of pleasure washes over my skin, and every nerve ending stirs and tingles. The feel of her sweet, hot sex taking me whole only makes me crave her more. I lick my lips and close my eyes. A shift near my heart echoes of the longing whispering through me.

I've dated and tried other women on for size, but the fit was always wrong. Riley and I have only been playing these roles for a couple of weeks, and I'm already anchored in her space, grounded by her presence. How can she feel this good? How did I get this lucky?

The sweet whimper that spills from Riley's full pillowy lips pulls my insides low and tight. It's imperative for me to taste her moan and feel her lips crushed beneath mine as I move inside her. I vary my strokes from hard and fast to slow, then glide out to the tip. We're both breathless, and our rhythm in sync. Again. Fast, slow, thrust hard and deep. Pull out to the tip only to do it all over again.

Riley moans and arches her back, baring her throat to me. I glide my tongue down the delicate column of her neck to the swells of her breasts, licking and sucking until her nipples are hard in my mouth. She clenches her thighs around me. Her hands are on my neck and in my hair, her hips winding me up as I plunge deeper. She opens wider, and I pump harder, faster until her muscles go taut. Her lips part, and her body is wracked with shivers and quakes. She gasps for air, falling fast and taking me with her.

As we lie there, our chests rising and falling in succession, I still don't know how we got here or if any of it is real, but I can't help but feel, maybe, just maybe, this time she let go.

CHAPTER EIGHT

The next day, I don't think about what a sadist I am for loving every heated second of last night and this morning. I'll worry about Monday on Monday. In the meantime, Chase and I do my favorite activity...activities. We stay in bed all Saturday morning being lazy, moving only when necessary for sex, food, and the occasional bathroom break. I'm like a kid on Christmas Day.

Speaking of, since it's less than two weeks until Christmas—one week until the holiday party—the movie marathons are in full force. We both prefer classic American comedy horror films that masquerade as holiday movies, like Gremlins, as opposed to the sappy ones where the people need to save the—fill in the blank—business, church, theatre, ski lodge. But, somehow, I feel more merry watching them with an amazing man who happens to know where to put his jingle bells.

And his southern mistletoe kisses.

"What are you thinking about?" Chase asks as he tugs on a pair of jeans.

I'm sitting on the foot of the bed grinning ear to ear because I've finally submitted my presentation to Spencer. Other than staring lasciviously at Chase Campbell, now known as sex god, showering and brushing my teeth with a toothbrush from one of his Costco bulk packs, I can't do much else. There are no cute Secret Santa outfits for me in his closet, so I'm watching *The Holiday*, living vicariously through Cameron Diaz, and watching her one-night stand with Jude Law turn complicated.

I'm right here with you, girl.

"Now I'm finally getting into the Christmas spirit," I say.

On the television, the ad for Bianca's Snowball Jam flashes across the screen with bold red and white themed script.

"Yeah?" Chase's voice is gruff and throaty like he's spent the night, and the better part of the day, filling up my frequent shopper sex card. "May I ask what sparked this new appreciation for all things merry?"

I peek over my shoulder at him and bite my lower lip because shirtless Chase may be a new world wonder. *We do not have time for another round.* "Oh, you know, just some office tryst with a hot coworker…"

"So, you think I'm hot?" He flashes me that cocky half grin that did it for me in the first place. My pulse races and already the dull ache between my thighs escalates to full throb. He must see the heat in my eyes or hear my playful growl because he stops mid-zip on his pants. "You're sure we have to go to this thing? If you ask me, Secret Santa parties are overrated. You buy a nice gift and inevitably come home with someone's perverted idea of a gag gift that you have to keep another year to regift."

"All this sensible, practical talk." I wave my hands playfully. "It's a turn-on, so just stop, or we're never going to get out of here."

I flop back on the bed.

Chase, I'm quickly learning, is never one to back away from a challenge.

"Buying toothbrushes in bulk saved me almost ten dollars." He shrugs and climbs onto the bed, softly brushing his lips over mine. "I also subscribe to Consumer Reports to get the best deals on appliances, vehicles, and other large purchases. Should I start talking about interest rates?"

We're definitely going to be late.

One more round of sex and two hours later, after stopping by my house for me to change and then at a convenience store for two holiday boxed wine sets, we're finally at Darrell's. The instant the door opens, Chase and I are whisked inside where it's jam packed and stadium-volume loud. We're stripped of our coats and immediately given a peppermint flambe shot to get us "into the spirit" as Darrell says.

Then we're turned loose into a throng of our coworkers in ugly sweaters—*missed the memo on that one.* I scan the crowd, but I don't see Nina yet. Thankfully, I haven't spotted Jessica, either. The tension in my shoulders eases slightly.

Chase leaves me for a few seconds to take our wine boxes to the gift table then he comes directly back to my side like I'm his protector. He twines our fingers and dips his chin toward my ear. "Don't leave me."

I chuckle, following his line of vision. "Are you afraid Evelyn and Renee are going to corner you under the mistletoe?"

Just as I say their names, my two least favorite marketing girls glare over at us.

"Ooh, we are pissing them off big time," I say, glancing around the room, unwilling to give them the satisfaction of a reaction. I'll bet it really burns them up that I have the audacity to be with Chase Campbell. What could he see in a girl with faux locs and all these silicone-free curves?

Suck it, ladies.

Chase squeezes my hand. "I have a few ideas how we can really make them jealous..."

I peek up at him and giggle. "Try to contain yourself for a few hour—"

He cuts me off with a kiss. His lips crash down on mine, hungry and ravenous as he dips his tongue between my lips.

"Fuck, that dress," he groans into the kiss as he tugs me flush to his body, his hands groping dangerously close to my ass.

In this short dress, that's a no-no.

I'm breathless when we pull apart. As much as just being near Chase electrifies my body, we are among people we have to see every day at work who also like to run with the slightest inkling of gossip.

"Bro," Craig bellows loud enough to drown out "Jingle Bell Rock." "Relax. We're going to get the gift exchange going here in a bit. Why don't you come help us out with these beers?" *Asshole.* As if he's crisis management, he turns his patronizing tone and douchey face to me with his palms pressing the air. "Riley, are you going to be good if he leaves you for a few? I know it's hard. My boy is a fucking stud."

A collective laugh rumbles over the immediate area. I have to fight back the urge to roll my eyes at him with his stupid red and green drunken llama sweater. "I think I'll manage," I say, flashing him a tight smile.

Of course, Nina materializes out of nowhere. "Girl," she says dramatically, ushering me off to the kitchen where she helps us to a couple of rosé coolers. "You guys hooked up, didn't you?"

"We..." My first inclination is to lie and save myself the heartache and embarrassment. It'll make the fallout smoother when—*if*— Chase and I put an end to this real fake relationship. Then Nina dips her chin to her chest and gives me the *don't even think about lying to me* look, and I know I'm going to tell her sooner or later, so it seems pointless to delay.

If Keira had come to me with this story acting like a lovesick puppy, I would tell her it was lust and nothing close to love before I'd proceed to tease her. And now here I am...

I nip the tip of my finger to stifle the grin tugging at the corners of my mouth. Then I nod.

Nina all but screams as she bounces on her toes. "Dammit! I knew it. Was it any good?"

I'm just about to come up with some lame story about how it

was "just sex" when movement out of the corner of my eye snags my attention. Darrell and Craig both fall to the floor trying to do some dumb alcohol-fueled trust game—which I could care less about. Everyone around them fumbles to get them up in a loud blur of movements.

Except for Chase.

He's leaning against the wall like a still-frame of masculine beauty with the etched lines of his broad shoulders, his easy posture, and his classic rebellious preppy charm. Every touch, stare, and sound we made together comes flooding back, and I'm homesick even though we're only feet apart. We've only sampled what it would be like to be together, and already I crave him...ache for him.

The look in his eyes when they meet mine is *very* inviting.

"Holy orgasm, my panties are wet just looking at you look at him," Nina says, biting her fist with a moan.

I'm so screwed.

I have to catch myself, but for a split second, I'm not thinking about Monday or how many ways this—whatever this is between Chase and me—can go so wrong. Instead, I'm in quicksand, sinking into the shamelessly optimistic and foolish idea that all we need is one solution—just one, and we can somehow spin reality. Maybe we can turn this sham into something safe and real, and maybe my little white lie to Spencer won't have been a lie at all.

When he pulls his bottom lip between his teeth and flashes me that sexy lopsided grin, it's not a stretch for me to think that somehow, some way, if we're together, we've got this.

MY GAZE IS FIXED ON RILEY AS SHE WALKS SLOWLY TOWARD THE BACK of the house then pauses to flash me an expression, I hope to God I'm not misreading.

"I'm going to take a leak." I fumble trying to set my bottle on the coffee table. Cock-blocking Craig curls his upper lip at me, his shoulders up to his ears like *fuck if I care.*

This dude is the worst.

I don't know where she went, but I'm stumbling down a hallway peeking in closed doors and feeling like I'm a teenager who's about to get lucky when I see the door to the backyard is open. It's dark and quiet, but there's a faint glow from an exterior light.

As soon as I step foot outside, Riley grabs me by my shirt, shuts the door behind me, and wraps her hands around my neck.

"I need you," she says, breathless.

Instantly, my dick throbs. It's one thing to kiss, but to go at it right here out in the open when anyone could walk out? "Here?"

Riley doesn't speak. Slowly, she releases her hands from my neck and starts unbuckling my pants. As she dips her warm hand under the waistband, my knees weaken. There's no way I'm going to say no. She wraps her hand around my girth, stroking until I'm fully erect.

"So, I don't have a condom..."

"I'm on the pill," she replies.

I groan at the feel of her stroking me. "Okay, if you're sure. My tests are good."

"Mine, too."

She lifts the hem of her dress and I'm trying not to come before we even get started. "You're sure about this because we can leave right now. I have your gift in my pocket."

Her eyes snap to mine, but again, she doesn't say anything. Her lips are on my neck, and if I get any harder, I'm going to break.

"I don't need gifts. All I want is you," she says, and that's it.

I lift her up against the side of the house and center myself before thrusting my hips. It may be the fact that we're outside in the cool air, or that anyone could catch us, or even just the feel of her without any barriers between our skin, but I'm wrecked. I'm ruined for anyone else.

It's not just our bodies, I'm consumed by Riley—light-headed and lost in the fit of us. I'm in tune with our breaths and our heart-beats. With every thrust, I'm deeper but never deep enough. The way she's holding on so tight, it's got to be the same way for her. I know I won't be able to let go.

And I *know*.

We haven't argued or been through any real skin-thickening times together. We've really only scratched the surface, but I'm certain like I know my own heartbeat, Riley is it for me.

Her breaths are fast and shallow, and it's probably not fair to say this while I'm still inside her, but my emotions are too urgent not to.

"I'm falling for you Riley."

She squeezes me, her fingers twisting in the fabric of my shirt as she kisses me with a relentless hunger. She's tasting me, moaning the whispers of her heart. Traces of light glint off her beautiful tear-stained cheeks.

"I'm scared, too, but I want this," I say. "With you."

Only the rhythm of our breaths echo in the air as I thrust deeper, faster, memorizing how good we are together and the feel of our emotions in motion. The friction builds kindling, smoking out our fire until her orgasm courses through her. She's spent and beautiful and mine. I keep stroking, every muscle in my body hardening until I come.

After a few minutes, I gently set Riley on her feet, but I don't erase the distance between us once we've straightened our clothes. I run the pad of my thumb over her swollen lips and replace it with mine.

At the sharp rap of applause, we both jolt. From the shadows on the other side of the yard, Jessica Faulkner's silhouette bleeds into the light. She plucks a cigarette from her lips, drops it, and twists the tip of her pink heel on the butt. "That was some perfor-mance," she says. "Phew, that was *hot*! Like new love but *four* years later."

"Fuck you, Jessica," I snap.

"No. Riley's got that territory covered." She flashes us a wide

71

grin. "You'll have to tell me and my husband your secret. We weren't even a year in before we stopped going at it like rabbits. Guess if I was a 'diamond in the rough' we'd have a baby by now, and I wouldn't be eating and sleeping my work." She shrugs.

Riley shifts into the light and the sympathy in her eyes is almost palpable. "Jessica—"

"Don't. I don't need your pity." Jessica pauses for a beat then snaps her fingers and points a finger gun at Riley. "But I will take that promotion. Should be nice to get a pretty sizable pay raise right here at the holidays."

I shake my head at her. "That's pretty weak that you have to eliminate your competition to come out on top."

She heaves a loud, satisfying sigh, and her arms hang limp at her sides. "You know I didn't think so before, but you guys are actually really cute together..."

Riley grits her teeth which only serves to widen Jessica's grin.

"Oh, and Riley, you were right about Eric Voorhees. He was fired for falsifying reports—lying, if you will. It's so _unethical._" Her smile is full-blown. "Ah, well. Guess I'll see you guys later. I'm going to go enjoy the party."

Jessica slowly walks to the door and lets herself inside. As the screen slaps against the frame, the sinking feeling in my stomach breaks me because I know she just took my only chance at happiness with Riley.

As if on cue, Riley's shoulders tense as she lifts her chin, but she doesn't meet my eyes. Everything about her is leaden and defeated as she says, "Can you just take me home? I'm not in the mood to party anymore."

I fish my keys out of my pocket and as my fingers graze her Secret Santa gift, uncertainty swirls in the pit of my stomach.

CHAPTER NINE

I take a deep breath and draw my shoulders back, tipping my chin up.

You've got this.

"Not for nothing, but if you let Jessica win, we're all doomed." Nina's draped over the wall of my cubicle with pouty lips and her baby face twisted in agony. "Don't do it, Riley. I'm begging you. Your coworkers need you."

"If I don't tell Spencer the truth, she will." I tug the lapels of my jacket tight across my chest and press at the crease of my black slacks. Through the glass, I see him sitting at his desk, still on a conference call.

The second he hangs up, I'm going in. I've got to get this over with. Jessica isn't going to hold this over my head.

"But doesn't Spencer think you guys are dating? Didn't he say to go to the holiday party together? This isn't the same as falsifying reports. It's your personal business. Who cares if Jessica's perverted ass saw you guys getting busy in the backyard? By the way, can I just tell you how proud of you I am?" She swoons and presses her hand to her heart.

I haven't seen Chase since the party Saturday.

The memory of us outside Saturday night floods my mind.

Longing whispers through me when I think how my skin had tingled as desire percolated between us. How my body ached for only him. But it wasn't *just* sex. In that stolen moment in the shadows, our hearts eclipsed, but lust blindsided me. I couldn't see it then, but we were aligned in every way a man and a woman could be.

My heart wrenches.

"What proof does she even have? I mean, did she record it? If not, it's her word against yours."

"That's not the point," I whine.

"Then what the hell *is* because I'm confused," Nina heaves a frustrated sigh. "You weren't at work, you're consenting adults, and no matter what the suck-up thinks, you and Chase are so freaking hot together. Don't let her throw shade on your parade."

"Actually, Jessica said we looked good together, too…"

A wave of dread washes over me as Spencer leans forward doing that smile-at-the-phone-because-I'm-about-to-end-the-call nod.

My stomach plummets because I've got to get to him before Jessica does. This was my idea. I can't hurt Chase.

I scrub my hands over my face and pinch the bridge of my nose. "This all started because Spencer James likes to promote 'sticky people,' remember?"

"Um what?" Nina's top lip curls and the crease between her brows deepens.

"At the all-hands meeting. Jessica was talking about how Spencer always grooms people who have reasons to stick around. You know, marriage, kids, mortgage. I don't have any of those things. Just a fake relationship with Chase."

"But that's just it. *You're* completely missing the point. It clearly isn't fake." Nina's tone is so sharp and matter of fact. The way she pins me with her stare, it's like she's a mirror, and there's nowhere to hide my feelings for Chase.

I drag my gaze to meet her warm brown eyes. They're filled with empathy as she softens her tone.

"You've got so much more to offer than your relationship status, Riley. What matters is, *you're* real…and ethical and a hard worker. Whether you've been in this relationship for two weeks or four years, it doesn't matter. He knows you're loyal, committed and, and you're innovative, dammit." She laughs. "That's who he wants working for him. A real person."

She rights herself and rounds the corner until she's in my cubicle. She stands at my side, and we both watch as Spencer replaces the phone receiver on the base.

"Be honest. If Jessica wasn't a factor, would you be telling me not to tell him? For me, this also has to do with my integrity. Lying to get what I want is not the route I want to take to advance my career."

Nina doesn't miss a beat. "No. But I'd also remind you what you have with Chase doesn't come along every day. It's what every single subscriber to Lovestruck and every other dating app out there is looking for. It's what Keira is looking for. Love. It's why it's a billion-dollar industry. Everyone wants love, but it is not promised to anyone."

The corners of my eyes sting as I swallow my words.

Do *I* love *Chase?*

Spencer swings his door inward and walks out of his office. He flashes Nina and me a quick smile as he walks past my desk toward web development, and I don't say a word. I simply let my chin drop and the tears fall.

AFTER WORKING THE WHOLE DAY WITHOUT TALKING TO RILEY, MY heart is in my throat. I thought giving her the space she needed to process everything that happened Saturday night was the right move—let her come to me first. She didn't, though. As far as I know, she didn't meet with Spencer, so all is not lost. Yet. But I can't let another day go by without talking to her.

This is why I'm outside her door, freezing my ass off with my heart on my sleeve at eight in the evening. I'm loaded down with Chinese, another batch of her favorite M&M Christmas cookies, and the Secret Santa gift I never got a chance to give her.

A whisper of a breeze sweeps through the trees as I ring the doorbell and take a step back, biting back a shiver. When the door swings open, a wave of warmth, light, and minty fragrance washes over me.

"Rile—" Her name dies on my tongue when a woman with rich brown skin and gold-flecked brown eyes appears in the doorway. She's taller and curvier, with a mass of textured curls instead of locs, but I immediately see the resemblance.

A smile breaks out on her face when I don't say anything else.

"She's indisposed at the moment, but I'm Keira, her sister. You must be Chase."

I'd be lying if I said her knowing my name didn't send a wave of warmth through me—it means, one way or the other, Riley's been talking about me. She hasn't forgotten me.

Yet.

Keira's whole demeanor is airy and welcoming, and even though I'm still on the wrong side of the door, the tension in my shoulders drains the slightest bit.

"Is it weird I just want to say, 'It's carolers,' like Keira Knightly did in *Love Actually?*" She laughs. "You're much cuter than that guy, though. Plus, he always makes me think of fighting zombies, so there's that, too…"

Keira's gaze drifts over me appraisingly, and her full lips quirk into a smile.

"Uh, yeah," I start, shaking the confusion from my head. "I'm sorry, I just… Do you know when she'll be available? I *really* need to talk to her."

My eyes dart past her into Riley's bright, relaxed living room, and Keira leans into my line of sight blocking my view before peeking over her shoulder. When she returns her attention to me, her eyes are narrowed, and her eyebrows pull down. She's got an air of defiance in the way she heaves a sigh.

"Look, if it were up to me, I'd let you in, and you two could kiss and make up." Her tone is gentle and careful as she dips her chin. "But Riley's my big sister, and even though I think she's crazy insane to let you go, she has too must dirt on me to even think about overriding her 'wishes.'" She air quotes the word and rolls her eyes playfully.

I'm listening, swallowing the emotion thick in my throat, ready to suck up my pride when she winks.

It's so off-putting, I freeze, unsure of exactly what is happening.

"Uh…" Tilting my head, I scratch my beard, and my posture loosens.

But Keira just stands there, her gaze darting this way and that, and I'm truly thrown. Her eyes widen like she's trying to communicate something, but it's gobbledygook to me.

My mind races, and I narrow my eyes, searching for answers.

Then Keira presses the air with her palms, nodding, before holding up a finger. Apparently, she's going to catch me up on this game of charades.

"So, as adorable as you are standing out there in the *cold*," she says super loud. "I know you're shivering and alone with those big puppy-dog eyes and all this *delicious food*…" she says, trailing off with another exasperated sigh and I catch on.

We have an audience. The woman who's taken my heart hostage is listening behind her, and we're making our plea without saying as much.

"And with Christmas right around the corner, too. It's a shame." Keira smacks her teeth dramatically and makes this tsking, cooing noise that is so hilarious I'm having a hard time keeping a straight face. "But I'm going to have to ask you to respect her wishes, too. Goodbye Chase. Best of luck to you."

Apparently, this is the end of her bleeding-heart monologue because she gestures for me to say something. She makes a pouty lip sad face and pretends to wipe away tears with her fists over her eyes. She wants me to milk this for everything it's worth.

Playing off her energy, I clear my throat and sniffle for effect. My voice is flat and monotone as I get into character.

"I guess I'll go watch *This Christmas* or *Elf*," I say, letting my shoulders droop, and bowing my spine. "Maybe I'll drown my sorrows in a vat of spiked eggnog." I have to cough to stop myself from both laughing and gagging. I'm halfway hoping Riley will hear the Christmas classics I'll be forced to endure and come out and save me.

"Be well," Keira says with the air of a seasoned thespian.

Rubbing a fist against my chest, I hold a hand up to wave and turn on my heel. "You don't have a tissue, do you?" I sniff again.

When I peek over my shoulder, Riley is at the door with her arms folded across her chest.

I choke back a laugh.

She's standing beside Keira, and there are traces of humor and sadness in her expression, but she flashes me a smile anyway. "You two are literally the worst. Useless, the both of you." She chuckles as she moves outside.

My heart gives a small lurch to see her in the sweatpants and T-shirt she wore home when she stayed over my house.

"What are you doing here, Chase?"

"Aside from freezing my ass off out here, I'm trying to bribe you with food and bring you the Secret Santa gift I never got to give you, and...I'm also here to plead my case." I laugh despite the heavy, hollow feeling in the pit of my stomach.

"Your case?"

The breeze picks up again and I flit a glance over my shoulder as a car passes by.

Keira shoots Riley a raised brow daring expression. Her lips purse, and her arms cross, letting on she's well aware of every-thing that's happened between Riley and me up until now. I'm just glad to have her on my side.

"Hear him out," she says.

Riley and I laugh because this is unexpected for both of us.

Even when she first conjured up the phony office romance, I couldn't have anticipated we'd be here now.

She sags against the door frame, her arms still folded across her chest and her eyes watery with indecision. "Listen—"

"Please." I set the bags of Chinese food—my only source of heat at the moment—on the pavement beside me and jam my hands in my back pocket. I've got to get this right. Dropping my chin for a beat, I close my eyes. "This was all supposed to be a fake relationship, I know, but somewhere along the way, it wasn't—it isn't. Honestly, I don't know that it ever was. Not for me."

I lift my head and meet Riley's soft gaze.

"So, I'm asking you not to tell Spencer. Not to stage our breakup when you get this promotion. Let's date. Please, let's keep exploring this amazing thing that fell into our laps."

"Chase, I can't. Where's my integrity if I lie to get a promotion? If I allow your job to be a risk because of it?"

Her voice hitches, and my throat tightens. My vision blurs as I nod, my mind warring with sadness and fear. To be so close to Riley and know I'm losing her, it feels like a knife to my heart. I'm devastated and desperate.

"I don't care if I get fired over a lie about a relationship that shouldn't matter when it comes to you getting this job. You're the best candidate. Period." I throw my hands up, begging her to see my perspective.

She just shakes her head.

"Listen, being at Lovestruck has never been about career growth for me, and maybe it should be, but I'm still more interested in learning about real love. *This*, what you and I have, nothing about it is superficial or run of the mill. I want the kind of love my parents had, and this is the closest thing I've experienced to it. I'd rather have you than this job, Riley."

She presses a hand to her eyes and wipes. It's killing me not to be able to go to her, take her in my arms, and kiss her pain away.

Her voice is thick with emotion. "I just can't let you do that for me. I'll make sure Spencer knows it was all me—that you had nothing to do with it."

"Why not? What we have is so much more important to me. I can get another job anywhere," I say, hating the desperation in my tone.

"But why should you have to? I'm the one who got us into this by lying. Chase, I'm not willing to hurt the ones I love..." she trails off and panic appears on her beautiful face. Her lips are parted and her eyes wide with surprise as she gasps.

She didn't finish her sentence, but that one word, those four letters, they're all I need to hear to know I'm not insane for feeling what I'm feeling.

My heart knocks around in my chest.

In one long stride, I erase the distance between us, cupping her face. Our lips are inches apart, and I'm breathless, but I have to say something first. "I love you, too." A smile tugs the corners of my mouth. It feels so good to name this feeling that's been welling up in my heart these past few weeks. "Riley Mills, I'm so in love with you."

Then, I let my lips crash down on hers. Every nip and lick and swipe of our tongues feels urgent, necessary. It's messy and complicated, like us. Heat curls down my spine, my body throbbing as desire radiates between us. She rubs her hands wildly over my chest, and it feels so good to know she's missed me, too.

I release a low growl, loving the way my skin blazes beneath her touch. She's jump-starting my heart the way only she knows how.

"Ew," Keira says good-naturedly, edging back into the house. "There is such a thing as public indecency. Take it to the bedroom."

We pull back from the kiss, and I'm laughing, but then I notice Riley's pained expression and the tears she doesn't try to hide. Her silence is deafening.

Humiliation burns through me. What I thought was a shared homesick hunger and desire isn't.

She cups a hand over her mouth. Her chin is quivering and her shoulders curl over her chest. Her posture is crumbling, and I know this was a goodbye kiss.

"Riley, please."

She reaches out to touch me then pulls back. Her voice cracks, "I'm so sorry. I can't do this to you." Then she steps back and closes the door on us.

CHAPTER TEN

As I cross the intersection, I double-check the address for the banquet hall against the small building tucked in an old shopping plaza on the south end of The Strip, before pulling into a nearly empty lot. The holiday party is supposed to start at seven, but I'm early. If I can catch Spencer before he ducks inside, it'll save me a world of trouble. *And one more heartbreak.*

Since there are only two other cars here, I relax for the moment, letting Bianca's upbeat version of "Have Yourself A Merry Little Christmas" temporarily lend a crutch to my mood while I survey this jewel hidden in plain sight. There's not much by way of neon signs and the glitz of glamorous casinos, but it's an architectural eye-catcher with charm to spare. Even parked two rows from the building, I see the quiet allure locals, tourists of a certain taste level —or sweet couples with *real* budding relationships—might be drawn to.

Let your heart be light…

Through the floor-to-ceiling grid of glass and steel, a holiday wonderland is framed in string lights. A tall, proud spruce tree with giant red bows and bulb ornaments grounds the room. Dressy accents and traditional holiday decorations bestow a touch of luxury. There's holly and garland accents with poinsettias and wreaths for pops of color. Though muffled, I can hear the bass from familiar holiday songs from outside.

I'm lost in the dream of Chase and me dancing the night away, loving each other without limits, and planning a future. But as cars begin pouring into the lot, I have to remind myself it is all just a dream. A fantasy, really, because sometimes protecting the one you love means those limits are there for good reason.

The driver's door of a red sports car parked directly in front of the banquet hall's entrance swings open, and Spencer is out and heading inside before I cut the ignition.

"Shit." I grab my purse and hop out of my car, taking long strides as I jerk the key fob back, arming the car.

The instant I step inside, I'm annoyed with myself for not parking closer. I got too relaxed while I waited, and this is the penalty. Jessica and her husband are already here looking like they're ready to be crowned king and queen of the small-town Christmas ball. They're holding hands and standing just off the entrance like unofficial greeters, so I flash them a small smile.

"Hey, Riley," she says. Her tone is surprisingly genuine while she introduces me to her husband—Troy or Roy, I think. I shake his hand and we exchange pleasantries, but I have to wonder if he's as much a wolf in sheep's clothing as his wife.

The way she judged Chase and me, I halfway expected her to have a trophy husband, but everything about him is very middle of the road—he's medium height, slightly balding, and average-looking. But he's got kind eyes and a sweet smile, so I have to wonder if she'll show her true colors in front of him.

"My wife talks about you all the time," he admits, but there's nothing sinister or gloating about his tone.

I force a smile and flit a questioning glance to Jessica.

Funny enough, I'm not as much surprised by her having a nice, vanilla husband as I am seeing Jessica in anything other than pink. She's on theme with a chic and easy red A-line dress with a furry white shrug.

"Nice meeting you. If you'll excuse me, I need to catch up with Spencer," I say, testing the waters.

In classic form, Jessica lifts her chin at the mention of his name, baring her delicate throat. There's a subtle gleam in her eyes, almost a warning, and I'm sure there's still a wolf underneath her dress.

"Oh, okay. We'll see you around," she says quickly. A smirk plays on her lips as her gaze darts behind me. "By the way, where is Chase tonight?"

I survey her, giving a small head shake because I know he's here, and I don't have the heart—or the stomach—to look at him.

Chase calls my name, but I'm already beelining for Spencer. Just as I reach our boss, Chase catches up to me and we're both standing there breathless and awkward.

"Ah, you made it." Spencer turns, his broad shoulders drawn back, chin high. He's holding a glass of bright-red punch, a perfect match for his festive velvet suit. "Listen, I had a chance to look over your report. I've been meaning to talk to you about our last discussion…" His eyes are filled with excitement and fixed on me, and I feel my resolve waning.

"About that," I start and stop, swallowing my reservations. "What I said in our meeting, about Chase and me—"

"You'll make a fine senior marketing manager, Riley." He smiles and it knocks the wind out of me because I wasn't expecting it. It's always weird to hear someone you respect say good things about you. Especially, when you're not all the way convinced yourself.

My mouth falls open, but I've lost my words.

"I've been observing your work ethic and sales strategies for some time now. The safety measures you've outlined…that's the kind of innovative thinking I need on my team, in my work family. You're a hard worker and loyal, and I have to say, I was pleasantly surprised at your initiative when you came to express interest."

I'm dumbfounded. Freaking flabbergasted. A burst of happiness suffuses my entire being. But then, there's still that sour taste in my mouth.

Is he saying this to me now because he's always observing, or did I just come to his attention since I fabricated a relationship out of thin air?

Spencer scrutinizes me for a moment, and I wonder what potential he sees in me—how he can speak with so much conviction when I'm questioning my own integrity.

I open my mouth to speak again, but he pats my shoulder. "Tonight, we're celebrating our work family and the season of joy." He leans in closer, "And secretly, your promotion. I haven't told anyone else yet, so I trust you two will remain tight-lipped until Monday. If at that time you still want to talk about what's worrying you, come see me first thing."

He walks away, lifting his glass in the air for a toast. "To St. Nick!" He cheers with loudmouth Craig who's in the middle of the dance floor in a Santa Claus costume complete with real fur and a fluffy white beard to boot.

The room erupts into yelps and howls just as "Christmas in Hollis" by Run DMC blares from the speakers. Naturally, Craig throws back his drink, sets the glass down, and starts doing an over-the-top worm on the floor, spinning out into breakdancing.

Chase, who's been quietly standing beside me the whole time shakes his head as a chuckle sputters from his lips, and I can't help but giggle too despite the weight on Spencer's words on my chest.

"Such an idiot." Chase laughs. His fixed stare on me lets on he wants to say so much more, but he's holding back, letting me lead.

When I raise my chin to him, all the humor drains from me. I'm about to say the first coherent thing that comes to mind when my attention snags on Jessica. She's dragging her factory model husband by the hand straight for Spencer.

I'M SO PISSED.

I could see it in Riley's eyes, she was about to say something important, something I want to hear. Then fucking Jessica Faulkner is on the move. I want to march up to her and ask what exactly her problem is. Why is she intent on ruining things for me with Riley? I know it'll fall on deaf ears, but also, she's already clinking a fork against her wine glass.

The deejay cuts the music. A collective hum rumbles over the group.

"Happy holidays everyone! It's almost Christmas," she announces. Her tone is all cheer—a little too much, but her flaring nostrils and jerky head movements give away her rage. "To keep with all the merriment, I have a little gift for you all, a bit of news you'll be interested to know about one of my favorite coworkers."

My body tenses because I know she's going there. I'm tempted to grab Riley by the hand and get her out of here and shield her from Jessica's messiness. I'm not sure she wants help—or anything —from me anymore.

Drawing my shoulders back, I clear my throat. "She's going to do it," I say to Riley, but I can tell she's already battening down the hatches, bracing for the backlash.

Her delicate shoulders slump. Her expression is blank as she sighs dejectedly. "Let her."

"Okay, then, I'm right here."

Jessica holds up a hand to quiet the crowd, stepping out of reach of her husband whose tight smile gives away his difference of opinion about her tactics. "Did you know we have a 'diamond in the rough' among us?" Her eyes and mouth widen with feigned awe. "She's bright and ambitious, dresses the part for the job she wants, works harder than everyone...a real rarity."

Riley lifts her chin as she and Jessica lock eyes.

"Her most notable quality? She's willing to do whatever's necessary to be the best." Jessica drops her chin to her chest and closes her eyes for a beat before looking up with a renewed determination. "But what if I told you it was all a lie?"

The palpable excitement wafting through the room morphs into gasps. While each and every person looking on could stop this right now, no one says a word. They look around at each other, scanning for signs of who Jessica's talking about, content to be onlookers rubbernecking the wreckage as it occurs.

"What if I told you Riley Mills and Chase Campbell were never in a serious relationship?" Every pair of eyes snap to us while she continues. "Not four years. Not two, but zero. They've flaunted themselves in front of us like a happy couple with their framed pictures, hand-holding, and lunch dates like they were—"

"That's quite enough," Spencer says, and a wave of relief washes over me.

People with any sort of scruples or self-control would stop at this point, cut their losses, and be content with the damage they've already inflicted. But Jessica Faulkner is not a normal person by any definition of the word.

"No, no. Spence, you definitely want to hear this."

I almost laugh at the murder in his eyes when she shortens his name, but the shitshow isn't over.

"I mean, I know we basically sell the promise of love for a living, but I'm pretty sure we mean the real stuff. Not some fabricated, watered-down, backyard, quickie version, right?" She's practically foaming at the mouth, reveling in this… performance. "Especially since she'll be your senior marketing manager. Is that what I heard you say over there in the corner, Spence? You're promoting her?" She laughs hysterically.

I scrub a hand over my face and rest my hand over my mouth.

"Congratulations are definitely in order." She slowly claps, egging on the crowd to follow suit.

Spencer pinches the bridge of his nose, and I'm guessing this villainous employee monologue wasn't what he had in mind for his "season of joy."

Come on.

"Now, it's important to note a few things." Jessica paces to the center of the room apparently playing to the whole crowd. *Heaven forbid someone in the back misses out on this insanity.* "We already know the 'what' and the 'who'—Riley and Chase in an allegedly

88

serious relationship. But, there's still the matter of when, how, and most importantly, *why*.

"Let's be clear, it was three and half weeks ago when our favorite boss announced this Christmas party."

Jessica goes on to highlight—with full courtroom movie dramatics and flare—the corresponding timeline beginning with her initial mention of promotions to "sticky" people. This is followed by her supposed supporting evidence. Riley's meeting with Spencer, both times she caught us making out, and Exhibit A, our notable separate arrivals to this party.

She takes measured steps over to Riley and me.

"So now I'm asking you, does their timely relationship seem like a coincidence, or the tactic of an *unethical*," her gaze drifts pointedly to mine for a beat, "immoral, overly ambitious woman who'll stop at nothing to move up in the company? Because I have to wonder..." She finally turns to face Riley whose watery eyes and silent resolve only make me want to touch her more. "Where is your integrity?"

My heart pounds against my chest. A war between anger and empathy for Riley wages inside me. I'll be okay with or without this job, but I know what she stands for is almost, if not more important to her than what she works for.

"That's about enough, Jessica," I say, unwilling to stay silent a second longer. My voice is sharp and full of bass, my jaw tight enough to snap. "Everyone is watching and waiting on edge. You've got them eating out of your hand. That's what you wanted, right? Well, I'm sorry about the struggles you and your husband have gone through but—"

"Stop it." Riley's red-rimmed eyes flit to me as she presses a hand to my chest. "Don't do that. Hurt people hurt people. She's hurting and taking it out on me, but I'm okay," she says, her voice is thick with emotion when she turns to Jessica.

"You're right," she says plainly, letting her words calm her nemesis for a brief pause before speaking up. "She's absolutely right. I wanted the job—still want the job—but I didn't think I'd be considered. As the most recent hire, I didn't have the tenure, but I have the degrees and so many ideas I can't wait to share." She laughs despite her tears. "Though my reason for wanting the job is driven by a personal cause, I never thought it was good enough. So, when Jessica mentioned most promotions were given to people with family or kids or people with reasons to stick around, I thought I had to have the same reasons as everyone else."

Jessica drops her chin, the fight draining from her.

"It was all my idea. Chase had nothing to do with it. It was wrong of me to lie, and I'm sorry." Her tears fall freely as she looks each person in the eyes before meeting my gaze.

I want to band my arms around her, kiss her hair and her eyes, tell her everything is going to be fine. But she's withdrawn, already far away. "I'm sorry. About everything."

Before I can stop, she steps into the opening with her chin raised. "You guys enjoy the party."

Then, for what feels like the last time, she slips away.

CHAPTER ELEVEN

"Faster!" Keira shouts from the other end of the rink. She and Nina have already lapped me. Twice.

I wave them off to keep going without me. My body's no more willing to move on this ice than it has been to drag me up off the couch since yesterday. It's Sunday, I'm nursing a broken heart, and I'll probably need to be in the unemployment line first thing tomorrow, so why not freeze my toes off while taking baby steps on this slippery death trap?

Oh, and it was the only way to stop my sister and best friend from nagging me since the crack of dawn. But, at least there's hot chocolate.

Over the loudspeaker, George Michael's voice blares "Last Christmas," and more people who know how to skate better than I do flood the ice.

Nina glides up beside me followed by Keira who scrapes up a flurry of ice when she skids to a stop.

"You have exactly five more minutes to mope," Keira asserts, making a big production of pushing her sleeve up to flip her smart watch in my face.

"I'm not. I'm skating. See?" I take one long glide along the edge of the rink then throw my hands up. "There. Are you happy?"

"No." Nina and Keira bark in unison.

I let my head hang back, blowing out a plume of cool air as I sigh.

"You picked ice skating." Nina says through a laugh. "If I recall correctly, you nixed baking because it reminded you of Chase. No cookie swapping. Same reason. Oh, and what do you know, no Christmas movies because you already did the movie thing with Chase."

I roll my eyes. It's been literally a day since I last saw him, but these two hard-asses have zero sympathy for me because "I brought it on myself." Or, so they say. Never mind the fact that I'm trying to do a good deed here, leaving him out of the lie so he can keep his job and integrity. How thoughtless of me to think of someone other than myself...

"Are we seeing a pattern here?" Keira chimes in as she dips her shoulder against mine playfully.

I groan and drop my face into my hands, pigeon-toeing my feet to keep upright.

Talk about embarrassing. I'm sure this is quite the sight to see for all these bundled up people trying to enjoy their Sunday evening on ice beneath a blanket of twinkling stars. Heaven forbid they want to do it to the soothing sounds of Nat King Cole rather than three women huddled off to the side of the ice yelling at each other. How am I supposed to deal with being woman-handled without face-planting in the process?

With one hand latched onto the wall, I hold the other one out to them. "What would you like me to do, go crawling back to him?"

"Nope," Keira says, spinning in a circle. "We're not doing that today. We're not making this about anything other than you and your fears."

Nina tips my chin up and taps her ear indicating that I need to listen close.

I am.

Usually, when I do the right thing, I feel good. Maybe not immediately, but after a few hours. The impact and implications of my actions are reaffirmed by a deep-seated calm. This hollow heaviness without Chase makes this time different. My heart is in my stomach, my chest aches, and I'm numb. If I did the best thing for him, why is this emptiness gnawing at me?

I meet my sister's warm brown eyes, this time not only with a willingness to hear her out, but to find something to take with me.

"Riley, you have to know that you hold people up to these impossible standards. Then you don't know what to do when they don't live up to them—or when they *do*. And that includes you."

Nina nods. "She's right."

I know it, too.

"So, you screwed up, told a little white lie about a relationship which turned out to be the best thing that ever happened to you. Yet, you're willing to throw it all away because of what people might think of you?" Keira shrugs. "I don't see it because anyone who has lived or worked with you knows your work ethic and integrity are indisputable."

Nina taps her index finger to her nose. With her wide, smiling eyes exaggerating the nail on the head, the three of us laugh. She's not here to instigate or give advice. She's reinforcement—the best kind of moral support.

She cozies into my right side, resting her head on my shoulder.

"Thank you." I heave a sigh of relief. Somehow, their unwavering belief in me releases some of the weight from my shoulders. "I just... My biggest concern is letting him get hurt because of me. I don't want him to lose his job because of a lie I told, you know?"

Keira slides to my left shoulder while people whiz by us. "I do, actually. Not that you need a reminder, but when I went on that date..." Her words die off, but I don't need to ask which date she's talking about. I was there in surround sound.

"I didn't listen to my gut." She drops her chin to her chest and absently studies her cuticles. "I should've left the second I saw he didn't match the picture—"

"It doesn't excuse what he did, Ke. You didn't do anything

wrong." It's the same spiel I've been giving her ever since that night—trying to convince her. *And myself.*

There wasn't anything I could have done to save her. A man nearly assaulted her while I was helpless, tuned in to every whimper, gasp, and yell for help.

"I know. My point is," she says, turning to me, her tone filled with conviction and urgency. "What *he* did wasn't a little white lie. He was intentionally deceiving me for malevolent reasons. When he cornered me in the restroom, I blamed myself for not listening to my instincts sooner." She blinks her tears. "And I know every time you look at me, or when I tell you I have a date, when you're at work brainstorming safety measures for the app, your mind keeps going back to that night, too. But you can't protect everyone, Riley. All you can do is listen to your instincts."

Nina pivots and skates in front of me, so we're face to face. "Forget everything else. If he's willing to risk losing his job for an amazing love with you, why are you fighting it so hard? Shouldn't he get to decide for himself?"

I drop my head back with a sigh before meeting her determined gaze again.

"What are your instincts telling you about Chase?"

The first tinkling notes of "All I Want for Christmas Is You" fill the air, and it's like a sign. Whether it's from the universe or the Queen of Christmas herself, Mariah Carey, I'm not sure, but I can't ignore it. My heart is so light, and something like joy bubbles up inside me. The corners of my mouth twitch with the beginnings of a smile.

"What was that?" Keira asks, starting to smile.

I clear my throat, trying to suppress the silly grin threatening at my lips. "Nothing. It's our song. Well, our favorite Christmas song."

"Who? You and Chase?" The corners of Nina's eyes crinkle then she tosses me a conspiratorial glance at Keira.

My sister nods, her whole face lighting up. "I see. So, you guys have a *song*. Sounds serious, like maybe this isn't some casual hookup, but an irreplaceable thing worth risking a replaceable job for."

She skates into the lane, turning backward. *Showoff.* Nina and I trail behind her while I do my best to ignore Keira's sparkling eyes.

"Let's just say, I'm not *not* in love with him."

Keira stumbles and her mouth falls open as she works to regain her footing. "Well, shit. Now that she's finally admitting what I already know. What in the hell are we still doing here? We have work to do."

"Ooh." Nina speeds up to Keira leaving me in their flurry dust. "I have *the* best idea. Think Christmas meets *The Proposal.* Add in some mistletoe, that cute red dress she has with the cutouts at the sides…"

I crack my neck and bite back a grin. If I'm going to let these two hopeless romantics plot my happily ever after with Chase with our jobs on the line as a grand gesture, they'd better at least warm me up with a cup of hot chocolate with whipped cream… heavy on the peppermint sprinkles.

"Two of whatever you've got on tap," Todd says as he settles on a stool at the far end of the bar facing the television screens.

I take the stool next to him, letting the weight of the past few weeks roll off of me.

It's the first time I get a good look at my brother. We're twins, but we're not identical. We're the same height, same lean frame, but his beard is thicker, fuller. His face is much thinner than mine. As far as work and home life, we couldn't be more different. Todd's married with a kid on the way and a career he loves and has control over. I know what I want, who I want, she just doesn't want me.

He slaps me hard on the back, laughing. "My baby brother finally has time for me."

This is what I need. I mean, my back is still stinging, but the playfulness is what I've been missing—along with, alcohol, basketball, and regular conversation.

"How's Kim?"

"Oh, you know Kim when she's got her mind set on something. The doctor says, 'Take a load off, kick up your feet, let your husband wait on you for a change.'" His shoulders shake as he chuckles.

I laugh, too, because my sister-in-law may be pregnant, but the second someone tells her *not* to do anything, baby in tow or not, it's a surefire way to get her *to* do it.

"Let me guess, she hasn't sat down for two seconds?"

"Exactly. Especially now that it's the holidays... Our house freaking looks like something out of Whoville. The other day, I literally had to take the ladder away from her. The lights she was going to string up were low-hanging, but, still..." He laughs a deep, throaty laugh this time.

His familiar snort leaks in and it tickles me, too.

A lot has been going on, but I miss my brother. I miss my family in general.

Todd must sense I'm thinking about mom. It could be the twin thing, but I see the hollow smile on his face, too. This was her favorite time of year. All the holidays were, really, but Christmas was special because she made it special. She put so much love into all the little details. When she wasn't baking, she was crafting, making homemade cookies and cards. There wasn't a room in the house not fully decorated for the season, filled with carols, and fragrant with the smell of cinnamon and pine.

I look up just as Brown throws an air ball on the television.

Todd pats my shoulder. "I miss her too, man."

"It's just this time of year. Seems like it hurts worse not having her around."

The bartender sets our beers on the bar top in front of us, and I quickly grab my glass and take a long pull before replacing it in front of me.

"At least you have Kim and the baby on the way. Pretty soon, you'll be too tired, up all night putting together toys at midnight before Rudolph and Santa jingle into town." I smile at the vision of the life we knew as kids, sneaking peeks and trying to stay up long enough to catch a glimpse of the old man in the red suit. "Do we know if it's a girl or a boy yet?"

"A girl," Todd says, taking a swallow.

"Oh, man, congratulations!" I pat him on the shoulder, feeling genuinely happy for him. Mom would have been so excited.

Then he twists on the stool to face me, his chin lowered to his chest. When he looks up, his forehead creases. "Chase, you know you're always welcome to come around. Kim would love it. We're always entertaining someone, but...what's going on with you? What happened with Riley?"

As soon as he says her name, my heart wrenches and my throat tightens. I scrub my hand over my face. "It's over."

"How can that be? I just talked to you a few days ago and you sounded like the heavens had opened up just for you. That doesn't just go away because you decide it's over." Todd cocks his head. His shoulders are lifted in question. He's begging me to make it make sense, but I'm at a loss here, too.

I suck in a breath and pinch the bridge of my nose. "She doesn't want me, man."

"I call bullshit." He tosses a glance at the screen as our team steals the ball and makes a drive for the basket. *Layup.* His gaze falls on me like a wall of sticks and stones. "For real, why do you think she doesn't want you?"

I spare him all the steamy highlights, but ten minutes later, I've ticked off the events of our brief timeline up until last night at the office holiday party.

"So, you're sure it's love? Like the Mom and Dad real thing?" Todd clarifies.

I nod, closing my eyes.

He just sits there bobbing his head, studying me in silence for a beat before throwing back the rest of his beer. After he jerks up two fingers to the bartender for a refill, the weight of my dilemma seems to set in fully. "Fuck." He runs his hands through his long hair.

"Exactly."

He doesn't let my news marinate long though. Todd rubs his stubbly chin a couple times then fishes his phone out of his back pocket with renewed purpose. He starts tapping away at the keys before pressing it to his ear.

"Who are you calling? I'm kind of in a crisis right now."

"Babe," he says into the line, and I deflate onto the bar top. Because of the noise in the bar, I can't hear her responses, so my brother's facial expressions are all I have to go by. "Yep. He's got it bad, too."

Really? You're doing this now?

Clearly, 'this stays between us' means something different to Todd, who's been spilling all my secrets to Kim. Damn spousal exemption.

I tell this man, my brother, that I'm in love and my heart has been efficiently shattered, and he calls his pregnant, Christmas-crazed wife to… "What is she saying?"

He holds me off, holding his hand up in the air as he listens to his wife. "Uh-huh. Yeah." He nods, repeating the same thing again. "So, does he take her at her word or…?" His question dies off, leaving me hanging out to dry.

I'm searching the familiar subtle differences of my brother's face, waiting for a throbbing vein or a nervous tick or maybe the corners of his mouth to hitch up in an optimistic grin. Sadly, for me, his poker face has always been better than mine.

The nodding and half-answers go on for at least five more excruciating minutes. By the time he ends the call, I'm on the edge of my stool with my pulse racing and heart revved up, hoping Kim has come up with the solution to my problem.

"Well…" I circle my hand in the air, urging him to come out with it. "What'd she say?"

My older brother by two minutes and forty-six seconds takes a deep breath, surveys his glass, and, finding it empty, polishes off the rest of mine before turning to me. "She came through. In. A. Big. Way."

I draw in a long breath, afraid to interrupt and make him lose his train of thought, but I admit, it gives me a warm, fuzzy feeling inside. Something like hope flutters inside me.

"Tomorrow's Monday. It's three days before Christmas, and you never gave her your Secret Santa gift, right?" Todd asks.

"Yeah."

He cocks his head to the side, scrutinizing me for a beat. "Do you still have the Santa costume from a few years back?"

I narrow my eyes, unsure of where he's going with this. Now I'm even more uncertain about taking advice from a woman hopped up on hormones and holiday cheer.

Todd's face splits into a smile. "According to my beautiful wife, it's time for you to 'put up or shut up.'"

My shoulders shoot up to my ears. "Meaning…"

"That's the girl version of 'shit or get off the pot.' Kim says you go all out at work tomorrow to win Riley back, or lose her forever." He grins like an asshole older brother. For years, I made fun of him for jumping in the Bellagio fountain to prove his love for Kim. Guess it's his turn to laugh.

"Apparently, it's all a test to see how bad you want her. The bigger the gesture, the bigger the reward. So, the way I see it, it's time to suit up, Santa." Todd chuckles.

Damn.

CHAPTER TWELVE

Through the glass, Spencer holds a finger up. He's still on the phone, but I don't mind waiting. I arrived early this morning. The whole two birds, one stone thing—catch Chase before he gets settled in then brace myself for the hammer to come down on my career at Lovestruck. But, since there's no sign of Chase and conference calls are starting earlier every day, I'm out in the open when people begin trickling in for the morning.

The hushed whispers and stares come first as people make their way to their desks. This is followed by heads slowly popping up over the cubicle walls like some life-sized whack-a-mole.

Finally, Nina shows up with her eyes wide to let me in on the details. "Jessica quit. My girl in HR said she sent her resignation letter Sunday morning." She squeals, her eyes darting over her shoulder. "The suck-up is gone. Word on the street is, she's going to iMatch with Eric Voorhees."

"Sure, she *would* leave right when I'm about to get fired."

Nina's peers over my shoulder before backing away to her desk, holding her hands up, fingers crossed. "Good luck."

I'm still smiling as I turn back to see Spencer replace his phone on the base.

He stands and gestures for me to enter.

Pushing the glass door, I duck inside, flashing him a shaky smile. "Good morning."

An empty feeling settles in the pit of my stomach. My mouth is dry, I swear I'm having heart palpitations, and for some reason, my senses are overloaded. All at once, I'm zeroed in on every tick of his small desk clock. His usually subtle musk cologne hits me like a smack to the face. Worst of all, the neon yellow folder on his desk is a blinding beacon, hypnotizing me.

"Riley?"

Spencer's voice snatches me out of my spiral. "Huh? What?"

"I asked if you'd like to have a seat?" He smiles that regal full smile and I settle into one of the sleek metal armchairs across from him. He sits, clasping his hands on the desk as he surveys me. "Riley, I'm still just another co-worker. No need to be nervous around me," he says, and it's like déjà vu—me in his office on the verge of doing something stupid, I'll later regret.

Then I breathe and flash him a small smile like I did that day. I remember Chase walking by, smiling sweetly and taking careful steps trying not to spill the two coffees in his hands. I'd been so jealous when I'd spotted one of them on Evelyn's desk...

"I'm glad you came this morning." Spencer flips open the folder and even from upside down I can read the word "offer" in bold at the top of the page. "Despite the events of Saturday night at the holiday party, I still feel you're the strongest candidate and the best choice for the senior marketing manager position."

"You do?" I feel my eyes widen. I have to hook my ankles around the chair legs to keep from floating away. "But you heard everything Jessica said. Chase and I were never together."

He leans back in his chair and again he searches my face. For what, I couldn't say, but there's a crease between his eyebrows and amusement sparkling in his eyes. And a... *Is he smiling?*

Spencer straightens and looks at me square in the eye. "Have I hired people in the past who've been in serious relationships with kids or dogs or mortgages? Yes. Did those people also have the best skills for the job? Also, yes. I'm not hiring you because you claimed to be in a relationship with Chase, Riley. You're the best person for the job."

It takes a full minute for me to let his words sink in. "So, you're not firing me?"

Spencer erupts into a deep base-filled laugh, shaking his head. "Is it always going to be this hard to convince you of what I'm saying? No, I was trying to *promote* you, but now I'm thinking maybe I should reconsider…" He laughs again.

"No. I'm sorry. I want the job."

I drop my head in my hands as it occurs to me, I'm getting everything I wanted. *Almost everything.*

"For the record, I've been in this industry a long time. It sorta goes with the territory to know the real thing when I see it. You and Chase may not have been together four years, but there was nothing fake about what I saw between you. There's no set timetable for love."

In the same way one person can say the same thing a hundred times without it resonating and another person says it once and makes all the sense in the world, something just clicks. What Chase and I had was never fake. Before the speed dates, I'd noticed him with the marketing girls and tried to ignore him. He even brought it up on our date. I'd never hated him…I just didn't want to be another member of his fan club. I wanted more than superficial conversation to appreciate him for his looks. I wanted a personal connection with Chase.

I run my fingers through my locs. I have this optimistic and foolish idea that all we need is one solution. Just one, and Chase and I can somehow spin reality.

"Uh, I know you just offered me the job, and I accept, but…" My heart is racing a million miles a minute. My chest tightens and I've got this desperate, manic energy, like I have to go to Chase now. I'm wringing my hands as I stand and edge my body to the door. "I have to—"

"Go. Tell him," Spencer says, but when I turn around, I realize I won't have to go far.

Chase Campbell is dressed head to toe in red trimmed with white fur and a matching curly gray wig and beard set. My mouth falls open as every person in the office forms a half-circle around a single table with two chairs and Chase at the center.

Slowly, I open the door of Spencer's office, flashing him a quick smile because he must've seen all this happening behind me while I was crumpled in a hot, desperate mess. I'm still not sure what the table and chairs are about, but I inch toward Chase anyway.

"Ho! Ho! Ho!" Chase announces.

A collective laugh rumbles over the crowd, and I shake my head. "What is all of this, Santa?"

"Please be seated." He digs in his pocket, coming up with a stopwatch as Nina weaves to the front of the group beaming. As I sit, I know without a doubt she and Keira have something to do with this.

Nina winks at me, confirming my suspicion.

"Eight minutes on the clock please, my little helper," Santa says to Nina as he takes a seat across from me and starts shooting rapid-fire questions. "What's the only Christmas cookie that matters?"

"Red and green M&M," I blurt out, laughing because this feels more like a quiz I'm being graded on than a weird speed date with a suspiciously sexy Santa Claus.

From a green velvet sack, he whips out a batch and slides it onto the table. "Name the best American comedy horror Christmas movie ever."

I scrub my hands over my face knowing the reaction I'm going to get from the crowd. "*Gremlins.*"

"Seriously?" I hear someone groan followed by another person whose voice has an uncanny resemblance to douchey Craig say, "I told you she was weird."

The man clearly knows nothing of the merits of watching Gizmo take down Stripe and the evil Mogwai.

Santa fishes the movie from his sack and slides it over, too. Four minutes and eight more kookie holiday trivia questions later, ten of my favorite Christmas things are stacked in front of me on the table. I feel like I'm on *Oprah*, except no one else gets anything.

"Two minutes, big guy," Nina announces.

He gives her a mock salute then pins me with his stare. "I have one request and one more question. You choose."

I nip at the tip of my finger, looking to the crowd for direction, to which half of them shout for the question and the other half for the request. I'm back at square one, so I take a deep breath, squinting my eyes. "The request."

Surprisingly, not from his magic sack this time, but from his inside suit pocket, he pulls out a pale blue envelope with the same bold red and white script I've seen flashing across the television. An ear-piercing shriek seeps out of me.

"Oh my gosh, Chase." I squeeze my eyes closed because if they're not tickets to the Snowball Jam, I'm going to be so let down. And if they are...

"Will you be my date to the Snowball Jam?" Santa Chase asks, and I'm so over this speed date and the dramatics.

I'm up off my chair, rounding the table to sit in Santa's lap. Before he can say a word, I yank down his curly white beard, letting my lips crash down on his to the tune of hoots and hollers.

"Didn't even take the full eight minutes," someone says.

"What is a Snow Jam?" another person asks.

But I'm so lost in the warm, welcome home of Chase's arms banded around me, I don't want to think about anything or anyone else.

"Don't you know, when the clock is ticking, you can't get to know a person by asking their favorite Christmas cookies and what movies get them in the spirit?" I ask.

He laughs a warm, throaty laugh that goes through me and pulls my insides taut. A ripple of pleasure sears through me.

We're staring at each other longingly because it'd be really weird and kind of awkward to go at it the way we want to in front of everyone. My heart gives a small lurch.

Nina clears her throat loudly. "There is one more important question," she says, widening her eyes at Chase.

"Right. Okay." He breaks our trance, but we don't move. A whisper of longing sweeps between us. "But first, to clarify, does this mean you'll be my date to the Snowball Jam?" He asks, running the pad of his thumb over my lip.

"Yes."

Chase takes a deep breath, swallowing then dips his forehead to mine and whispers, "Riley Mills, I love you with every fiber of my being. I would do anything for you to make you happy." His gaze falls to our fingers twined together. "You don't have to say it now, but do you love me, or think maybe you could grow to love me, too?"

He's so adorable with his big, stormy blue eyes as he waits for me to validate his feelings. There isn't a doubt in my mind how I feel about Chase Campbell. How could I not love him? How could I have thought I'd ever be whole without experiencing this all-consuming love? I fell for him the first four minutes we spent alone at the Mix'n'Mingle, and I've been falling ever since.

"Chase Campbell, you don't have to convince me. We may have started out in a fake relationship, but nothing has ever felt more real. I'm so in love with you."

I guess I'm officially the president of the Chase Campbell Fan Club.

EPILOGUE

The jumbotron illuminates as Bianca hits the beginning notes of her Christmas anthem, "Mistletoe Memories." The arena goes wild. It's loud and raucous as they sing the anthem. Of the thousands of people cheering and whistling, I've only got eyes for one.

"Mistletoe memories of just us two." Riley throws her head back to belt out the last word before turning to serenade me. *"Baby, no matter the season, I love you."*

She shuffles toward me with her arms outstretched. As I pull her flush against my chest, we rock back and forth to the beat. Riley peppers soft kisses on my lips, working her way behind my ear and down to my throat and I groan, closing my eyes.

"Hey. Be good," I say.

She pouts. "You're no fun, Santa."

I twist her around in my arms so her back rests against my chest. I tighten my grip and nuzzle the delicate curve of her neck. "We'll see about that tonight. I'm putting you on the naughty list."

Riley giggles, squirming against me, but I feel the slight shift of her body. Her shoulders tense. She's been keeping a watchful eye on Keira all evening. We first met Keira's date, Thomas, at the restaurant before the ball. He's average height and stocky with close-shaven hair…decent looking. There's really nothing threat-ening about him so far, but Riley had her guard up. Out of respect for her sister, though, she remained tight-lipped, keeping her judg-ments to herself—well, between us.

"Are you doing okay?" I ask.

Her response comes in the form of a squeeze to my forearm.

"I'm really proud of you, babe. I know how much your sister means to you." I kiss her hair. "You're doing the right thing letting her make her own decisions."

"Is it just me, or does their chemistry…does it feel off to you?" She blows out a sigh, and I know it's killing her not to be able to give Keira advice. "I hate it, but I know she's got to learn to trust her own instincts."

Bianca kicks it up a notch, bouncing across the stage.

Riley and Keira both break out into screams, jumping up and down as they sing along word for word. Both of their hands are in the air, swaying side to side, and my girlfriend is absolutely radi-ant. Her locs are twisted up in a ponytail and she's wearing her trademark red dress and matching lipstick.

Thomas shoots me an amused look like he's wondering how he managed to get talked into this. I won't tell him I volunteered, or that many Christmas-crazed people are jealous of us since it sold out—including a very pregnant Kim.

A laugh bubbles up inside me. It's a mix of nostalgia for the past and for the future. I miss my mom, but I love what Riley and I are building. Christmas Eve, Riley visited her parents and sister, and I spent the day with Dad, Todd, and Kim talking about the baby and starting new holiday traditions. That sort of cemented it for me. I want real love where you sit around with your other half planning a future full of holidays and vacations. I want to make real, lasting memories with Riley.

When Riley and Keira wind down, Riley finds her way back into my arms.

The mic crackles to life, and then Bianca, who'd twirled off stage, reappears in a glittering red gown. She tucks a long curl behind her ear and blows the audience a kiss. "Merry Christmas, Las Vegas. I just want to take a few minutes to thank you for spending your holiday with me. I want to dedicate this next song to all the lovers out there."

She takes her time singing the silky harmony of "I'll Be Home for Christmas."

Riley clasps her hands behind my neck and softly brushes her lips over mine. "I got you something," she says between kisses.

"Hmm?"

"Well, two things." She pulls her lower lip between her teeth and pins me with her stare. "I'll let you choose. Have you been naughty or nice, Mr. Campbell?"

I flit a glance over at Keira and Thomas, who are singing along.

"That depends." I seek and find her lips, devouring her mouth with sweeping strokes of my tongue. "How much longer is this Snowball Jam?"

Riley kisses me back, but she's smiling as her mouth moves against mine. When I pull back, her eyes are hooded with heat pooling in them. "It's Christmas, and I may or may not have gotten one of those naughty Mrs. Claus outfits you mentioned." Her lashes flutter up at me, sending my pulse into overdrive. My cock twitches. "It has bows and comes with a reindeer whip."

Defenseless against her tactics, I take a deep breath and step back, needing the distance between us to think clearly.

She laughs a warm, musical giggle as her eyes dart to the growing hard-on tenting my jeans.

"You know you're wrong," I say with a breathless chuckle. "That's just dirty when you know I can't do anything about it here." I crack my neck and bob my head. "Okay, let's go with nice. Door number two has got to be better."

All the light-hearted humor drains from Riley's expression as she erases the space between us. "Well, I've been thinking about us. Actually, a lot about us." A smile quirks at her lips.

I gently rub her back, urging her to continue, but also still nervous about getting too close, lest we have an inappropriate situation at a family concert.

"Chase, I know it's kind of soon, but..." She fishes her hand into the small clutch clasped to her wrist and pulls out something silver. "I was hoping you might want to make our own holiday tradition. It's an ornament. I thought maybe it could be the first in our collection together. Every year, we'll get a new one to add to our tree."

Our.

Every time she says that word, I feel my hopes rising and my spirits soaring.

With my free hand, I tenderly pluck it out of her palm. My insides flood with warmth as I examine its inscription.

The Two of Us.

"You never know what we'll be celebrating next year," she adds, a soft smile tugging at the corners of her mouth.

My heart gives a small lurch as I bite down on my bottom lip. "I love it, Riley, and I love you." Emotion clogs in my throat. "So much, it scares me."

She stands on her toes, kissing away a tear that's slipped free. "I'm scared, too, but in the best way possible. I know without a doubt I want a future with you, Chase Campbell."

As we hold each other, swaying to the music, joy wells up in my heart at the future she's painting for us. I want it all—the bright, vibrant colors of every season, the laughs and pranks. Every moment.

As long as it's the two of us.

*Thank you for spending your time with Riley and Chase. If you enjoyed Mingle All the Way, please consider leaving a **review**.*

Keep reading for an excerpt from Married & Bright.
See what happens in Vegas when a pop star wakes up married to her Rideo driver...

Join me in my reader group. I'd love to chat! That's where I connect with readers most.
Mia Heintzelman Reader Group

AN EXCERPT FROM THE NEW - MARRIED & BRIGHT
CHAPTER 1

Airports are so weird. *Especially*, during the holidays. You start out in the terminal hefting around too many bags to fit the length of your trip. You're tired and anxious to get into a car and then on the road. As you make your way to passenger pickup, some rendition of "I'll Be Home for Christmas" is playing overhead. Instantly, you're nostalgic as your path is littered with Christmas trees and gigantic wreaths shoved between slot machines. Then, you step out to into the parking structure and it's *The Shining*.

Breathe, Bianca.

The sun is already low in the sky, making it feel darker and colder. My ears tune in to every voice and tire screech on the upper levels.

The automatic doors behind me swish open with a whoosh of cool air, giving me a start. When a pilot dragging his suitcase walks out, I try to settle my nerves, but my pulse is thumping. He dips his head in a small nod as he crosses the economy bus pickup on his way to employee parking.

And I'm alone down here again.

My heart is beating a mile a minute, but I guess this is what I get for letting my manager, Damien, plan "inconspicuous" transportation. *This is definitely low-key, Dame...and creepy.* I'm standing curbside on the dark commercial level at arrivals waiting for lord knows who, when a candy-apple-red sedan pulls up in front of me. I tighten my grip on the key wedged between my ring and middle fingers.

The driver lowers the window. I take a deep breath and lean down to look inside.

A slim, clean-cut, nerdy white dude with a Dexter haircut is at the wheel. He's in his mid-thirties. Just the type to get away with some *Bone Collector* taxi abduction shit in a sketchy-looking part of the airport.

His thin eyebrows slowly crease as he does a double take. "Rideo for Zoey?" he calls out to me in a questioning tone.

Immediately, I heave a sigh of relief, letting the knots in my stomach unravel. "That's me," I say, bending down to gather my tote and backpack.

Technically, it's not me, but you can't just broadcast on an app, "World-famous pop star, Bianca." It would be mayhem. Anyway, to avoid certain doom, Damien always gives me a celebrity name based on whichever TV show or movie he's obsessed with at the moment. I should've known after he binged three seasons of *New Girl* last night, it'd be a toss-up between the character Jess or the actress Zoey.

Strangely, I *could* break out into a random song right now. Though, it probably wouldn't have quite the festive ring to it considering I'm just happy to be alive right now.

"Zoey? Did I say that right?" the driver asks, still staring.

His eyes drift over me. He clearly knows who I am. The baseball cap, leggings, sweater, and boots I'm sporting—all black—are standard uniform for dodging paps at LAX. But I'm not in La La Land anymore. This is McCarran airport. Vegas, baby—and all that entails—where you don't turn a blind eye, and you call a spade a spade.

"Let me—" He starts to get out of the car to get my suitcase, but I ward him off by holding my hand up in the air.

"I've got it." I shove my tote and purse into his spotless backseat. "Happy holidays. Thanks for picking me up. I can't wait to settle in. I'm exhausted," I say, tossing him a tiny smile meant to put a cork into the small talk.

He just ogles unblinking at me with his big brown eyes while I fumble with my giant suitcase. The man obviously recognizes me, but lucky for me, he seems intent on playing it cool—if only for a great rating and a tip worthy of a recording artist whose Christmas single is at the top of the charts for the fifth week in a row. *Woot! Woot!*

When I'm settled in the back with an audible harumph, he fires up his sensible hybrid electro-engine. At some point, he mumbles his name, but I'm not really listening because I'm too busy watching the road to make sure he's going in the right direction.

Dammit, the creepy parking structure is rubbing off on me.

Either way, I kind of like referring to him as the "Bone Collector." I'm sort of a stickler for not making people say their names twice.

B.C. weaves out of the terminal and onto the freeway, fiddling with the music once he's merged onto the 15. I'd like to say I'm surprised when he selects my song, "Mistletoe Memories," but I'm not. Everywhere I go, it's playing on repeat.

"You know, she's going to be playing at T-Mobile Arena at the Snowball Jam Christmas Day," he says, as if I tapped his seat and asked, "Hey, who is this singing?" Hints of a Midwestern accent rumble around between his words.

I'm curious, but I don't ask because he's still watching me, daring me to admit I'm Bianca and not Zoey. It's like a weird test, and he's committed to dying on this hill, which is just creepy.

Let it go, guy. Let it go.

Every few seconds, B.C.'s gaze flits to the rearview mirror and lands on me like he's checking to see if I'll sing along or outright state my identity. Forget the whole famous pop star bit. As far as he should be concerned, I'm just another fare using a rideshare app to get home safe for the holidays. He should keep his eyes on the road ahead.

As if on cue, my phone pings, saving me from a fatal rearview mirror staring contest. I hunch forward and fish it out of my back pocket.

Low and behold, it's Damien. *No surprise there.*

Damien 5:28 pm
Rest your voice and keep a low profile. I'm working on THE gig
that's going to take your career to the next level.

I try not to put too much weight in Damien's words. If it's what I think it is, I don't want to get my hopes up. Tugging at my cap, I peek up. Again, B.C.'s gaze flickers up to the mirror, so I dip my chin.

Bianca 5:29pm
I haven't been home in five years. Unless Museik calls to offer me
the tour, do refrain from calling me, please.
New Girl
Lol. I'll see you at the Snowball Jam in two weeks.

As much as seeing Mom and the house will inevitably bring the heavy memories flooding back, I just need to get away and not think about my next album or my career or where it's going next. I just need family and…hot chocolate with extra whipped cream.

And sprinkles.

A little less than half an hour later, I incline my head to discover, thankfully, my final destination is not a deserted building but the cute, single-story house with about a million string lights and a huge blow-up snowman on the lawn. It's the house where I grew up—a*nd left as soon as I got my first recording contract.*

The weight of being back here after so long away, settles in the pit of my stomach. *You can do this.* I take deep breaths, peering over to the house again.

I'm sure Mom is waiting by the door, so I scramble to get all of my bags out. Then B.C. wedges his body between the two front seats.

He looks at me with expectant eyes as I step out to the curb. His pensive expression catches me off guard. The defined lines of his face harden like he's weighing what to say.

Curiosity twists inside me.

The unobstructed, head-on view of him paints him in a different light—a much brighter, less creepy one. He could still be a good-looking serial killer who now knows where I'm staying, but there's a softness to him. He looks a little concerned and a tad bit bashful.

Because I'm such a headcase, I am naturally drawn to it.

"Yeah?" I prompt, urging him to say it.

His lips part, and his breaths are shallow. The whole delicious sheepish look is about as contagious as watching someone about to sneeze. I lean in, breathless to hear what he's got to say.

"I..." He swallows, and there's a slight shift in his shoulders like he's considering his next words. Then, he releases a breath and drops his chin. "Nothing, I...I was just going to say, if you need another ride, you can favorite me in the app...if, you're going to be around."

For a split second, I'm ransacking my mind trying to figure out what he was going to say before he decided not to. Suddenly, I can't tear my gaze away from his pouty lips.

Oh, my God, why am I staring so hard?

"Yeah, okay. Thanks."

He's cute in an adorable, nerdy sort of way, but he's my Rideo driver.

When I close this door, I'll likely never see him again. Which is just as well. I'm only here a couple of weeks, during which I plan to hide out with Mom and pack in as much holiday fun as we can before I'm hopefully off on a world tour. *It's for the best.* I'm guessing a hookup with Bone Collector on holiday isn't what Damien meant by "lay low."

So, I pat the roof of his car and lean down. Despite his sweeping dark lashes and a decidedly strong chin, I tell myself it's just my dusty lady parts having a nostalgic knee-jerk reaction to a cute guy.

Before I do anything stupid, I toss him a small smile. "Thanks again, and happy holidays." Then, I close his back door.

I don't even look back until he turns the corner.

"STUPID. SO *STUPID*."

Why didn't I just ask for her number? Maybe we could've had drinks. I could have tried a little more conversation to see what she had planned for the night. I groan. How many times have I heard about rideshare drivers flirting with passengers and cringed in disgust?

Ah, it's not like I'm free tonight, anyway.

I blow out a breath, shaking my head as I hook a right at the corner headed for the freeway. It's Wednesday. My cousin Denise is probably two cocktails in already at Shane's, the off-Strip bar where she gets loaded on a weekly basis. She's a casino cocktail waitress Friday through Tuesday, so this is her weekend. Lucky me, I get to be her on-call chauffer to make sure she makes it home safe.

In the Brooks family, not showing up isn't an option.

When I make it to the freeway entrance, of course, the westbound lane is still bumper to bumper with the rush hour traffic. *Side roads it is.*

A few minutes later, when Denise's name lights up on the dashboard, I answer on Bluetooth. The cabin of the car fills with muffled background noise— mix of music and chatter.

"Hey. I should be there in like twenty."

"Don't rush. Lena's here." Denise slurs. *Probably two whiskey sours by now.* "It's jam-packed tonight."

"All right. You hungry?" I ask, hoping to help her soak up

some of the alcohol. The last thing I need is an accident in here. I just got my car detailed. "It's no big deal. I can grab you a quick bite—"

"No, I'm good for now. Just come hang out with us. Take a load off for *once*. The band is so *intense*. They're doing Christmas favorites."

I chuckle, trying to reconcile the image in my head of a hard-core grunge band singing cheery holiday songs. Then my mind drags me back to Zoey and how stupid I must've sounded using the Snowball Jam to drum up conversation. The commercial plays every hour on the hour.

A blaring horn startles me as a black truck speeds past.

"Yeah, all right... Okay, I'll be there soon."

For a few seconds, I think Denise hung up on me, but her name is still on the dash and the muffled music from the bar is still play-ing. "D?"

"Jaden, what's wrong with you?" she asks. "What happened? Why are you so distracted?" I can already imagine the alcohol-fueled wheels in her head spinning out.

"Hmm?"

"You're just going to have drinks with us without me begging? Obviously, something's going on."

My shoulders tense, and my pulse revs. Denise is like a fun-sized bloodhound with her goth black hair, bold red lipstick, and unmatched bullshit radar. She knows how to sniff out the slightest change in the air.

Better to tell her now, rather than in a bar full of people.

"It's nothing, really. You know how it is. All night it's been dead, right? Then, *ping*, an airport pickup." I slap the steering wheel. "Figured I had time before rescuing you, to make a little cash. Except, she was—"

"I knew it. You're totally crushing on your passenger!" Denise squeals, cutting right to the chase. "Was she interested?"

The light up ahead turns yellow, and I slow to a stop.

"That's the thing. There might have been *something* there... I just didn't feel right asking for her number. That feels like crossing the line. Doesn't it seem sleazy to you, flirting with a passenger?"

Denise ignores everything I just said. "Let me guess...a typical Vegas club girl with the plastic boobs and lips?"

"No." I release a short bark of laughter. "When has that ever been my type? This girl was nothing like that at all. I mean, she was at the airport, so she was dressed for travel. Maybe Latina... average height...not too skinny, but fit...curly hair in a ponytail and light makeup... It was more than looks, though. There was something more in her eyes. She seemed warm...genuine."

When Denise doesn't say anything, I listen to the muffled bar sounds.

In classic Denise form, she brings our conversation to a halt to recap my dilemma to her friend. I hear every word, though—their sarcastic tones while they debate my "textbook party foul," how I'm too much of a "decent" guy to take any risks.

My blood boils a little because maybe I would be more carefree if I wasn't always looking out for others and for family. Maybe if I wasn't worried about some trash dude slipping her a rufie and having his way with her, I might be out with friends on a weekday, or joining a beautiful woman in my backseat instead of staring at her like "decent" guys do.

As I pull into the small parking lot on the side of Shane's, Denise and Lena are still in my ear debating the merits of good guys versus hot bad boys. They've forgotten I'm here.

"Denise?" My tone is sharp.

There's rustling as she comes back. "Oh, shit. I'm sorry—"

I abruptly press the button to disconnect. It doesn't have the same effect as slamming a phone down and letting the dial tone echo in her ear, but I end the call feeling vindicated.

The way I see it, the score is: shit-faced cousin, zero, "decent guy," one.

Get MARRIED & BRIGHT Now!

ACKNOWLEDGMENTS

Happy holly merry days. Thanks for going along on this ride with me. Hopefully, you snuggled up with a warm cup of something cheery and whizzed through Riley and Chase's story. That you chose my book in which to spend your time is my honor.

This time of year when the season officially changes and we make memories with family is my favorite. Thank you to my husband, Daniel Heintzelman, who has allowed me to leap because he's my net, supporting me.

Shout-outs, hoots, and hollers to my writing family, my IG family, the librarians, bookstagrammers, bloggers, and reviewers. Thank you for enjoying and sharing my story.

To my editors, Danielle and Danylle, I'm indebted to your polishing skills.

Big hugs and smoochie kisses to my family and friends. You are the petals on my flowering tree and the frame holding up my house. You understand and support me even though I'm always with my nose stuck in a book or with my fingers glued to a keyboard spinning tales.

As always, Mommy and Daddy, I love that I'm equally introverted bookworm and (semi-)social butterfly. Thank you for always cheering me on.

My sister, Melissa DeGrazia, let's keep leaping in faith together!

Finally, to my two daughters and my nieces and nephews, I hope my daring pursuit of greatness is inspiration and wind beneath your wings.

ABOUT MIA HEINTZELMAN

Mia Heintzelman is a polka-dot-wearing, horror movie lover, who always has a book and a to-do list in her purse. When she isn't busy writing fictional happily-ever-afters, she is likely reading, or playing board games and eating sweets with her husband and two children. She writes fun, unforgettable, more than just laughs romance about strong women and men with enough heart to fall for them.

Website:
miaheintzelman.com

Subscribe to Mia's Newsletter:
miaheintzelman.com/newsletter.html

Join Mia's FB Reader Group:
Facebook.com/groups/2219575585012649/

facebook.com/miaheintzelmanauthor

twitter.com/miaheintzelman

instagram.com/miaheintzelmanauthor

goodreads.com/miaheintzelman

bookbub.com/authors/miaheintzelman

amazon.com/author/miaheintzelman